A KILLER AMONGST US

A gripping thriller, full of suspense

MARK WEST

Best wishes

Mark W

THE
BOOK
FOLKS

Published by The Book Folks

London, 2023

ISBN 978-1-80462-112-7

www.thebookfolks.com

For Sarah, Chris, Lucy and Milly,
With thanks that our walks in the gullies are a lot more fun
and nowhere near as dangerous!

Prologue

The man ducked out of sight behind a tree as Jo walked slowly along the path.

She seemed frightened and was clearly looking for someone. That was good. He liked the idea of her being scared.

He moved slowly around the trunk and stepped on a twig. It snapped with a report like a pistol shot that seemed to echo around the woods. He was annoyed at himself and how he could have been so stupid but at least it startled her.

"Martin?" she called but her voice wavered. She tried again and shouted his name this time.

She scanned the trees near to where he crouched and he held his breath. The sun was behind him, so he knew he'd be in shadow but now was not the time to get careless. Not when he had her right where he wanted her. She looked out over the gully on the other side of the path but it was too deep for her to risk going into.

When she started walking again he followed her and kept far enough into the treeline that she wouldn't be able to see him in the gloom. He could see her panic was mounting and she seemed jittery. He deliberately trod on another twig and she physically jumped at the sound.

He liked that.

She paused to look up and down the path. He stopped and his foot nudged something. He risked a quick glance and saw a large branch lying in the undergrowth. Stooping down, he picked it up. It was about three feet long and had a good weight to it.

The man smiled. This branch would be an ideal weapon.

Jo started walking again after taking another quick look around. He kept pace with her and didn't care if he trod on anything that gave him away because each noise seemed to spook her more.

"Martin?" she called.

The man hefted the branch as he walked. They were close to the hut and he needed to make his move soon. There was a gap in the treeline a few feet away and he decided that was the place. He stopped when he reached it. His heart raced at the thought of what he was about to do.

Jo came towards the gap slowly. Once she was level with him, he rushed out and swung the branch hard and fast. It hit her in the side and the impact jarred his arms even as it unbalanced her. He heard her breath whoosh out and that excited him. He swung again and this time caught the side of her head. She staggered back towards the edge.

One more hit would do it.

He swung for her face and her head whipped around as she dropped out of sight into the deep gully.

Chapter 1

It was a cool Thursday morning in late April.

Jo Harper sat in the passenger seat and turned from watching the Northumberland moors flash by the window to look at her husband, Martin. The sun was in his eyes and he wore the cheap red sunglasses Olivia had brought him back from Spain last year as a joke. He did look silly in them, even he acknowledged that, but because they were a gift from his daughter he used them all the time.

He glanced at her. "You okay?"

"I'm fine, how're you?"

"Currently looking at a sight even more stunning than the scenery."

"Yeah, yeah," she said and looked back out the window to hide her grin.

He laughed and rubbed her thigh and she enjoyed the heat of his touch. It was something that had been sadly lacking for the past couple of months and she'd missed it. So had he, it seemed, since this short break was his idea.

The first stage was a guided hike across the moor with an overnight stay in a tent. The weekend itself would then be spent in a luxury five-star hotel with a spa and the promise of good food. That part she was excited about, the hike less so. She enjoyed walking, she enjoyed the countryside, but couldn't remember ever being a big fan of camping. He reminded her they'd gone away a lot in the early days and enjoyed it and she decided not to point out they were ten years younger then and she'd long since lost interest in roughing it. A good shower and a nice bed were what she expected now if someone suggested going away.

But this was a chance for them to be a couple and Jo knew it would be churlish to complain. He was making an effort and she was more than happy to do the same. Plus, the hotel looked magnificent on the website and the Tripadvisor reviews suggested it was even better in real life.

"Thank you for agreeing to this," he said.

She looked at him again. "Thank you for booking it."

"We're going to have a good time, Jo." He pushed the sunglasses up onto his forehead. "It'll be good for us to get away from Hadlington and out into the fresh air and all that space. You'll love it." He curled his lip, and shrugged. "We'll love it."

"I'm still not sure about the tent," she said. They hadn't seen what they'd be using as it was included as part of the fee and would be handed to them when they reached the overnight camping spot. She made sure Martin ticked the 'roomy, two-person' option.

Jo had taken him to a Mountain Warehouse shop the previous weekend so they could have a look at the various models. She hoped their tent would be on the larger size of those she'd seen. She'd also picked up a new waterproof jacket that was bright purple and very snug and comfortable. When she told him he wouldn't lose her in it she expected him to laugh but he didn't and instead looked sad for a moment. She'd let it pass then because it harked back to the way things had been and she didn't want that feeling to linger.

It took them both a little while to get used to the idea of being empty nesters when Olivia left for the University of Exeter last September. Jo missed her stepdaughter terribly and Martin was like a man with the wind taken out of his sails. Things got better as the weeks went by but they didn't embrace this new chapter of married life as well as Jo had hoped they would.

Martin worked as a project manager and a couple of months ago, he'd begun a new contract that took up a lot of his time. So much so that she found his focus and attention often wandered, even if they were out enjoying life. He would be easily distracted, occasionally snappy and seemed to spend a lot of time on his phone. He was a practical man who'd always taken his work seriously and she respected that, but now it felt like a wall was slowly being put up between them and with the changes at home it seemed like the last thing they needed.

Jo was the more emotional of the two of them and tended to get a little more anxious about things than her husband. She worried that his recent behaviour was down to him not dealing with Olivia leaving but when they talked about it, he blamed work. The job was under-funded, he told her, and far too complicated for the timing plan they'd been allotted. There was no reason to disbelieve him and she'd never known him to lie to her but, by the same token, she'd never known him to be this removed from either her or their marriage.

But now wasn't the time to get herself lost in this melancholic swirl of thoughts. He'd happily suggested this trip as they came home from visiting Olivia in Exeter and they were both in a good mood because she'd settled really well and seemed to be having the time of her life.

"I know things have been a bit weird recently with work and everything," he said. "I should never have let it impact on us like I have and it's not fair. I know this weekend won't be like a magic wand making everything better but I hope it puts us on the right track."

"I hope so, too."

"There's been a lot of stress," he said.

"You could have talked to me about it before it got on top of you."

He gave her a quick tight smile. "Do you always tell me when you're stressed?"

"Not always," she said quietly. Over the years she'd developed her own little arsenal of tricks and tended to rely on them. Martin meant well but sometimes he didn't listen as hard as he could and his advice was occasionally 'don't worry about it', which wasn't helpful. She was happy to balance herself.

"Well you should, love, and, in future, I'll be more open."

"That sounds like a plan," she said.

The lift in his mood pleased her and she wanted to share in it and enjoy it. She watched the moorland whip by the window but, despite her best efforts, her mind drifted back to last week.

Now wasn't the time to wonder if she'd done the right thing by not telling him about her confrontation in the car park of the swimming pool or how terrified it had made her. Now was the time to work with her husband to strengthen their marriage.

Chapter 2

A high stone wall shielded Hadley Hall from the road and the grand building only came into view when Martin drove through an ornate gateway and up a short drive. A three-storey mansion with a mansard roof, tall windows and wandering ivy stood at the head of a gravelled area as if demanding attention. Several cars were parked and a minibus was close to the front door.

"Wow," Martin said. "That doesn't look too bad at all, does it?"

"It really doesn't," Jo agreed and decided it was probably worth a night in a tent.

Martin looked pleased with himself. "Glad you like it," he said and pulled into a parking space facing a wall.

Jo got out and stretched, then walked around to the back of the car. Martin opened the boot and pulled out their weekend suitcase and she took out the two rucksacks she'd packed for the hike.

"The email said we were to put the case in at reception," he said. "Do you suppose we just take them in?"

"I don't know," she said.

A man wearing a fleece and cargo trousers got out of the minibus. He was tall and broad with close-cropped blonde hair and a strong jaw. He waved at them.

"He looks like Action Man," whispered Martin.

Jo answered with a smile and waved back.

The man strode across the gravel and extended a hand. "Morning folks," he said. "Are you the Harpers, by any chance? Here for the Irchester Flow tour?"

"We are. I'm Martin and this is my wife, Jo."

"I'm Ross," he said and shook Martin's hand then hers. He had a firm grip. Up close, his face was weather-worn enough to make it difficult to guess his age – he could have been in his mid-forties like her, or younger. He glanced at the suitcase. "We'll get that away into reception and then load the rucksacks onto the transport, if that's okay?"

"Certainly," said Martin.

As if they'd been waiting for their cue, a young couple got out of a beaten-up Fiesta on the other side of the car park. The woman looked to be in her early twenties, perhaps not much older than Olivia. She was slim and athletic and her jacket and trousers fit her snugly. She had thick eyebrows and lushly red lips and her hair was styled into a pixie bob bleached almost platinum. She looked as if she was trying too hard and Jo felt instantly terrible for thinking it. As the woman opened the back door and pulled out two rucksacks, she caught Jo's eye and waved. Jo waved back.

Her partner was tall and thin and his pale red hair was tucked under a Detroit Tigers cap. His jacket looked old and careworn and his cargo trousers were bright red. He looked to be about the same age as the woman.

"Fellow hikers, do you think?" Martin asked.

"I assume so," said Jo.

"I think that's a fair guess," Ross said and raised a hand. The woman waved back as the young couple crossed the car park.

"Are we part of a big group?" Jo asked.

"Not really," Ross said. He was watching the woman as they waited for the newcomers to join them. "It's just three couples, which is the perfect size for this kind of hike. It means you can hear what's being said without feeling like you're in the middle of a crowd."

Martin's fingers brushed hers and he took her hand. The gesture gave Jo a warm feeling. They'd always been a tactile couple and that was another of the things she'd missed in the past few months. She squeezed his hand and he returned the gesture.

Ross introduced himself to the young couple.

"I'm Sam French," said the younger man. He shook Ross' hand then Martin's and Jo's in turn as they introduced themselves. "And this is Gayle Hill."

The young woman cast him an annoyed glare. "I can introduce myself, you know," she said. He looked at her aghast as she shook hands. "I'm Gayle."

She had large, beautiful green eyes, Jo noticed. "It's nice to meet you, Gayle," she said. Gayle had rings on every finger of both hands except her ring finger.

"I'm sorry," Sam said. "I do it without thinking."

"I'd maybe try to think a bit harder," suggested Martin.

"You might live longer," said Ross. "Is your case still in the car?"

"What case?" Gayle looked confused.

Sam looked a bit embarrassed. "We're not staying," he said. "Bit too steep for us, so we're just doing the guided walk."

"We could have stayed here?" Gayle asked.

"It was expensive," he said to her quietly.

Martin gave Jo's hand a quick squeeze and she recognised the sympathetic gesture. Things had been tough for them financially when they first met. He was a struggling single father and she'd just come out of a bruising divorce that had pretty much left her with nothing.

"Not a problem," said Ross quickly. "Shall we go?" Without waiting to see if they were ready, he turned on his heel and walked away. Martin and Jo followed him and she noticed Sam take his mobile out of his pocket and hold it over his head.

"I can't get a signal," he moaned as they reached the minibus.

"That's not unusual," said Ross. "There are blackspots all over the place here and on the moors. The hotel had to put in its own booster." He pulled open the back door of the minibus and gestured at the space. "If you put your rucksacks in there, I'll go and drop the case in at reception."

Martin put their packs into the space then moved out of the way so Sam could stash his and Gayle's.

Ross came out of the hotel talking to a much older man of medium height who was wearing a battered jacket and knee-length cargo shorts. His legs looked thin and wiry and his feet were huge. They came down the steps together and Ross was tapping a clipboard.

"Do you think that's someone from the other couple?" Sam asked.

"Hardly," said Martin. "He looks like he's on his last legs."

"Bit harsh," Jo muttered, though she thought he might be right.

The older man came around to the back of the minibus. He was somewhere in his sixties and the condition of his skin showed that he'd clearly spent a lot of time outdoors. He had a thick mop of white hair and sparkling eyes that looked full of good humour.

"Hello," he said. "I'm Peter Roth and I'll be your guide for the Irchester Flow hike."

Jo hoped the surprise didn't show in her face. She'd expected Ross to be the hike leader because he looked far fitter. Martin's expression suggested he felt the same. Sam and Gayle didn't speak. Jo shook his hand and introduced herself.

"Lovely to meet you," Peter said then moved along to the others. He didn't seem fazed at their reactions at all and she wondered if he experienced it a lot.

"Pete's the best guide you could hope for," said Ross. "What he doesn't know about Irchester Flow isn't worth knowing."

"I'm sure," said Sam.

Peter rubbed his hands together. "If we're ready," he said, "we should think about getting going."

"Hold on," said Martin. "Ross said there were three couples on the hike. Shouldn't we wait for the others?"

Peter looked at his watch. "We can hang on for a bit but can't leave it too long. I need to give us plenty of time to reach the camping spot so we can get set up before it's too dark."

"They're cutting it a bit fine," said Ross.

Peter checked this watch again as if to make sure he'd read the time correctly. "I reckon we could give them ten more minutes at a push."

"I don't think you want to be hanging around waiting for latecomers, though, do you?" Ross asked.

"Not really," said Martin. "But maybe they got caught in traffic?"

"Ten more minutes then," said Peter agreeably.

Ross loaded his rucksack into the back of the minibus. Sam moved towards the hotel checking for a signal and Gayle went with him. Jo leaned in towards Martin.

"Why are you so keen to wait for the other couple?"

"I'm not keen to wait at all," he said with the slightest hint of indignance. "But if we'd got caught in traffic I wouldn't be happy to get left behind. It's not fair."

"But they're the ones who're late."

Martin nodded towards Sam. "I know but look at it from another point of view. If that other couple don't turn up then we're going to be stuck hiking with Lanky Lad and his blonde bimbo of a girlfriend, aren't we? Did you want that?"

Jo shushed him and looked at Gayle. The young woman looked back with a dismayed and hurt expression. "I think she heard you."

"Oh well," said Martin.

The comment was out of character but before Jo could say anything a car sped in through the gateway. It sliced across the gravel and came to a skidding halt in front of the hall. The driver's door opened and a man got out quickly and waved towards them.

"Hey," he called. "Are you the Irchester Flow group?"

"We are," Peter called back.

"Phew," said the driver. "I was worried I'd missed you. I got held up in traffic."

"See?" said Martin.

"And then I couldn't get a signal to ring you."

Sam held up his own phone. "Same here."

"I did tell you," muttered Ross.

Jo felt a little frisson of recognition as the newcomer closed his door. The man was tall and broad-shouldered with thick dark hair. She knew him, she was sure of it, but couldn't quite place him.

He took a rucksack from the boot and pulled on an old green parka with a mod target logo on the back. He was wearing jeans and walking boots that carried years' worth of scuffs. He slammed the boot shut, shouldered his pack and came towards the group.

"Sorry," he said to no one in particular and made a beeline for Ross with his hand outstretched. "I'm Tony Newman."

Ross shook his hand then pointed to Peter. "This is your walk leader."

"Little older than I expected," said Tony, "but okay." He shook Peter's hand.

Ross checked his clipboard. "Is your wife still in the car?"

Tony looked confused for the briefest of moments. "No," he said. "Unfortunately, she's not been very well so she won't be coming along."

"I'm sorry to hear that," said Peter.

"Yeah," Tony said. "Gastroenteritis. Nasty business." He glanced at Martin and Jo and introduced himself. "Is it just us lot?"

"Us four, plus Sam and Gayle."

The younger couple came towards the minibus and Tony looked them over. His gaze settled on Gayle. "Oh this could be a nice distraction," he said.

"I doubt your wife would think so," said Jo quietly.

Tony grinned at her. "She doesn't mind me window shopping."

Jo felt her cheeks flush with embarrassment at being caught out. Tony seemed to examine her for a moment too long then his grin softened into a smile and he looked away.

She looked at Martin who shook his head lightly.

Ross directed Tony to put his rucksack in the back of the minibus then clapped his hands. "Okay, ramblers, let's get rambling."

Chapter 3

"Is that your boyfriend?" Tony asked Gayle. He'd moved to stand very close to her and Jo watched as the young woman hugged herself. Tony clearly made her uncomfortable and either couldn't see it or didn't care.

"Yes," said Gayle.

"What's he doing?"

"He's trying to get a signal," said Jo and took a step towards them, feeling protective of the younger woman and imagining Olivia in the same situation. They were heading off for an overnight hike and she didn't want Gayle to be on edge the whole time because the man clearly wasn't respecting her boundaries.

Tony glanced at her. "Oh right," he said then turned his attention back to Gayle. "So why's he so keen on a signal?"

"He's been filming some bits and pieces and wants to get them onto his cloud account."

"Aye, aye." Tony smirked, as if he'd already decided what Sam had been filming.

"Not like that," said Gayle.

Ross pulled open the sliding door on the side of the minibus. "If you'd care to get aboard," he said.

Tony held out his hand for Gayle and, with a nervous smile, she took it. He moved as she stepped into the van and Gayle made a strangled sound. Tony held both hands up. "Sorry, love, my hand slipped."

He offered his hand to Jo but she didn't take it and climbed in herself. There were double seats behind the front ones and Gayle sat in the middle one at the window. She looked up as Jo made her way past.

"You can sit here if you want," she said.

"Won't Sam want to sit with you?"

"I doubt it. He'll be sorting his camera out."

Jo turned to see if Martin was following her but he was talking with Tony. She wondered if Martin had recognised him too. "Fair enough," she said and sat down.

Martin raised his eyebrows in surprise as he got on. Jo gave him a little shrug and he sat on the seat behind her. When Tony got on he smiled widely at Gayle then sat on the seat in front of them.

Peter opened the passenger door. "Come on, Sam. We're going."

Sam gave him a frustrated look then trudged to the minibus and got in. When he saw Jo sitting next to Gayle his frustrated look grew worse as he plumped into the single seat behind the sliding door. He grabbed his rucksack from behind him and put it on his lap to unzip it. "Still couldn't find a signal," he muttered.

Peter knelt on one of the front seats to address his charges. "Okay, ladies and gentlemen, we're going to head off. As Ross said earlier, the phone reception is mostly dreadful on the area of the National Park we'll be walking on so you can leave your mobiles in the bus if you want. Ross will ensure they're kept securely in the hotel for your return."

Jo had no intention of leaving hers and nobody else volunteered theirs either.

"Fair enough," said Peter. "Just thought I'd offer."

"There must be some reception, surely?" Sam asked.

"You might be lucky but it's really patchy," said Peter. He settled down and faced the front as Ross got in and started the engine.

"Everyone ready?" Ross asked, then drove across the car park and turned left onto the road.

Jo looked out the window at the breathtaking views. The moors unfurled around them, a patchwork quilt of colours separated by stone walls and hedgerows that led to a ridge which almost seemed to touch the clouds.

She glanced over her shoulder, but Martin didn't see her as he was staring out the window himself. She watched him for a moment then looked towards the front of the minibus. Tony was looking out the window, his chin in his hand, and Peter and Ross seemed to be in deep, quiet conversation. She noticed Ross look at Gayle in the rear-view mirror and whatever he said to Peter made the older man turn around for moment. He saw her watching him and, for a moment, Jo was sure she saw a spot of colour in his cheeks as he quickly turned back.

She wondered what Ross had said to him but then Tony leaned forward to talk to Peter. She looked over at Sam. He was busy searching through his rucksack and his cap was draped over one knee. His hair looked messy but she could see it was markedly thinning.

"So what do you do for a living?" Gayle asked. She was sitting on one leg, her back to the window and she looked intently at Jo.

"I run the purchase ledger and credit control for a small tooling company in Hadlington."

"What does that mean?"

"I put invoices onto a computer system then pay them. I also do some debt chasing too."

Gayle's eyes widened. "Debt chasing? Like being a private detective or something?" Her enthusiasm was infectious and made Jo laugh.

"No, I basically ring companies up to remind them to pay us."

"And what happens if they don't?" It seemed like Gayle had already concocted a scenario in her head of Jo sending in the heavy mob.

"I tell them they won't get the parts they ordered."

"Oh." She sounded deflated.

"It's not very exciting but it's a steady job," Jo said. "How about you?"

"Oh, I'm not very exciting either but I think I'm relatively steady."

That made Jo laugh. "I'm sure only one of those things is true."

"You're too kind," said Gayle. "I'm doing hair and beauty at college and working in a salon in town for a couple of days a week and over the weekend. It's knackering but I'm really enjoying it."

"People will always want make-up and their hair doing."

"That's very true. Yours looks very nice." Gayle leaned in closer. "Do you mind?" she asked and brushed some of Jo's hair away from her shoulder. "What colour is it?"

"Ash blonde, or so it says on the box."

"I would've said that was your natural colour."

"It was once but I started finding grey in my late thirties so for the past few years I've had a little help."

"You're never in your late thirties."

"You're a darling," Jo said with a flush of warmth. "I'm forty-five."

"Wow, you're older than my mum." Gayle said it with the same kind of youthful enthusiasm that Olivia sometimes got caught up with, where they'd say something inadvertently bluntly only to be surprised to find they'd caused offence.

"Now you're just chipping away at my goodwill," Jo said sarcastically.

Gayle looked concerned. "I didn't mean it like that. It's just that you're a bit older but she's been colouring her hair for years. The last time I saw her it was lilac and not a subtle shade, either."

"I'm not brave enough to go lilac."

"However brave she is, it doesn't suit my mum at all and I told her but she didn't listen."

"Older people rarely do," said Jo with a smile to show she was joking. "So what drew you to this? Was it the hike or the thought of camping out overnight?"

"Neither to be honest, but I've started an Instagram account and Sam says it would be a great way to build up my following." She leaned forward. "He said the scenery would be spectacular and that'll help me get some attention and likes."

"What's your Insta about?"

"Tips and tutorials on hair and beauty mostly. Some of it is me doing things to my own face, some of it is work I do on my friends. I'm also trying to get into the influencer side of things, by doing promo work for other companies. Sam's a YouTuber and he's been giving me some ideas, like this trip. Going on a hike on the hills will play havoc with your hair so I found this little place online that does these gorgeous knit beanies. I got them to send me a couple of samples and he'll take pictures of me wearing them so they get exposure and I get associated with the product."

"Good thinking."

"He thought so. Do you have Insta?"

"I have an account, but I don't post much to it."

"We should follow one another."

"I'd like that."

"Great. So did you come along for the hike or for the pamper at the hotel? I wish Sam had told me about that. I mean, I know we couldn't afford it but it would have been nice."

"I don't mind the hike, but I haven't camped out since Martin and I first met, about ten years ago."

"Oh, that's lovely. Is it your anniversary?"

"No, he just suggested it out of the blue."

"That's so sweet," said Gayle. "Relationship goals and all that. So do you have any children?"

"Just the one. Olivia's my stepdaughter and a lovely young woman. Not much younger than you, I'd imagine. She's in her first year of university so Martin and I are empty nesters and just getting used to it."

"Are you finding that adjustment a bit hard to make?"

Jo looked at her. It was as if Gayle had read her mind. "A little. Why?"

Gayle smiled. "Because I think I would. Change is difficult at the best of times, but with your child going away I think it'd be ten times worse."

"Yeah, something like that. You're very perceptive."

"Thank you, Jo. It's just a thing I do. My tutor says it's the perfect attribute for the job, because I'm always sticking my nose in and I'm a good listener. She says a hairdresser is a free-of-charge therapist that a lot of people use without really being aware of it." Gayle pulled her sleeve up slightly to reveal a string bracelet. "Plus I've had my own issues with stress and anxiety."

Jo was impressed with her forthright admission. "A lot of people try to hide that kind of thing."

"It never does you any good."

"No, I know." She'd only known this young woman for all of five minutes but there was something in her demeanour that made Jo think she was trustworthy. "I've had a few issues, over the years. Olivia leaving home was one too. A friend of mine is a reiki healer and she talked me through the concept of mindfulness. I found it was a great help."

"Oh, it really is," said Gayle. She touched Jo's forearm lightly. Her nails were well manicured and nicely painted. "Everyone gets a little anxious sometimes but I used to think it was paranoia."

"Yes, me too." It had taken Jo a long time to understand that concept and this was the first time she'd had it validated by someone.

"You should use one of these stress bracelets. They're very good."

"I'll have a look for them."

"I can help you there." Gayle reached into an inside pocket and pulled out a small leather pouch. She opened it and took out a string bracelet. "I make my own and sell them on Etsy." She held the bracelet by the wooden bead on it and Jo could see it had 'G' printed on it. "You're welcome to take it, if you want, as a gift. But I'll understand if you don't."

"No, that would be lovely, thank you."

Gayle placed the bracelet carefully in Jo's palm and smiled widely. "There isn't a right or wrong way to use these but I find it helpful, sometimes, to stroke the bead. It's kind of like those fidget spinner things from a few years ago." She laughed. "And now I've ruined the mystical element of it."

Jo smiled and put the bracelet on. "Thank you for this. I'm sure it'll help."

"I hope so. I've found it useful because I struggle some days more than others." She leaned in conspiratorially. "My mum often says I overshare but I think that's partly because she's not all that interested and partly because my issues embarrass her. If I am oversharing, please tell me to shut up."

"Not at all."

"I think you're being too kind, but thanks. I find mindfulness helps me to focus because I sometimes feel like I'm lurching from one place to the next with no set route in mind."

"But you clearly do have one, because you're doing your studies and you've got your Insta."

"I used to do a lot more, Jo."

"Like what?"

"Well it's a bit of a tale." Gayle smiled shyly and ran a hand through her spiky bob. "I was at university but it got a bit overwhelming and I crashed and burned."

"I'm sorry to hear that. What were you studying?"

"Psychology."

It wasn't at all what Jo had expected and her surprise clearly showed.

"I didn't always look like this," Gayle said and made a vague gesture at herself. "Back then I was that girl that nobody really noticed, you know? The one with mousey-coloured hair and sensible skirts who tried to keep up but couldn't. It was only when I stumbled that I started to change things around."

"I think you look fine."

"Thank you." Gayle sounded as if she genuinely meant it. "You'd be surprised how many people take one look at me and form an instant opinion." She glanced quickly at Martin. "I heard what your husband said."

"Oh," said Jo. "He didn't mean…"

"No, he probably did," said Gayle, companionably enough. "Opinions are made quickly and I understand that. But the way someone sees me is their issue and not my problem. That took a long time for me to figure out."

This young woman was going up in Jo's estimations. "It's something that normally comes as you get older," she said. "You're the only one who really knows you."

"Well, I felt like I'd let myself down. I loved the course and the people on it but something didn't quite fit together in my mind and I couldn't deal with it so I dropped out." She blew out her breath. "So now I practise mindfulness and I'm studying something I'm interested in and I'm making me better." She mimed gagging. "I know that sounds ridiculous and I hope to get back to the psychology stuff, but I feel more on an even keel now. I realised I like helping people."

"There's nothing at all wrong with that."

"I wish my mum thought more like you do. She said I'd never stick to the course and she was right but I managed to rise above her comments. The only person who understood was Sam and he just let me get on with it and we kind of fell in together."

"That's how it happens, sometimes. And you're both doing things you want to do now."

"True, except that he's trying to shape my online presence into a similar style as his and I feel like we're drifting off that same page. I can feel things starting to brew up, if you know what I mean."

Chapter 4

Ross turned off the main road onto a narrow lane where twisted, heavy bushes scraped the sides of the minibus before giving way to dry-stone walls. Over them Jo could see miles of rolling countryside and a lone buzzard hovered over its lunch.

Rob brought the minibus to a halt.

"Why's he blocking the road?" Gayle asked.

Peter opened his door and jumped out and rushed around the front. He disappeared behind the wall.

"Where's he going?" Tony asked.

"Not far," Ross said over his shoulder as he steered into a narrow driveway. From this angle, Jo could see Peter was unlocking a padlock on a wide metal gate set into a wire fence. There was a wood beyond but a large sign hid a lot of it from view. The sign was stamped with a Ministry of Defence logo and appeared to be a list of items she couldn't read properly because she didn't have her glasses on. The warning at the bottom of the sign was printed large enough to be clear.

"Danger unexploded ordnance?" she queried.

"What the hell?" asked Sam. He leaned forward. "Where did you see that?"

"On the sign."

Ross turned in his seat. "Don't worry about it, folks, but we're on MoD ground. Unexploded ordnance means old bombs but the areas are clearly marked."

"We're hiking through a minefield?" Martin asked.

"That doesn't sound like a good idea," said Gayle.

Tony shifted to put his arm along the back of his seat and gave her a greasy smile. "Well, we've been driving with a bomb," he said.

"Yuck," said Jo but Tony ignored her.

Gayle acted as if Tony hadn't spoken. "Will we be anywhere near these bombs?" she asked Ross.

"No," said Ross in a tone that suggested he answered this question a lot. "Peter will explain everything when you disembark."

Peter pushed the gate wide open and Ross drove through a short way then stopped. After Peter closed the gate and re-attached the padlock, he got back into the minibus.

They went down a slight incline and the woods spread out on the right-hand side. At the bottom of the incline was another big metal gate. Peter got out and opened it and Ross drove through onto a gravel strip that cut between the trees. Through the windscreen Jo saw a large hill dotted with clumps of trees, bracken and rocky areas. Almost at the top of her vision was a large earth mound with a wide stony ridge next to it.

Ross turned off the engine and got out. He walked around to the back of the minibus and opened the doors. Peter pulled open the sliding door on the side of the vehicle.

"Okay, hikers," he said. "We're here. Everybody out."

Tony pushed himself off the seat, gave Jo and Gayle a big smile then got off. Sam stood up and put his camera in his rucksack before following Tony. Jo went next with Gayle behind her and Martin brought up the rear. Once they were out she pulled him close to her.

"I don't remember it saying anything about bombs," she said. "Did you know about them?"

"Of course I didn't," he said testily, as if it was the stupidest question he'd heard in a while.

Ross handed out the rucksacks.

"Thanks," said Jo as she took hers.

"Not a problem," he said and glanced at Peter. "Mrs Harper read the sign," he said.

"Of course," Peter said and took a couple of steps away from the minibus then turned to face the group. "Okay everyone, welcome to the start of the hike."

"What's this about bombs?" Martin asked.

"Yeah," said Tony. "I don't remember that in the brochure."

"It was," said Sam. Tony glared at him and Sam suddenly found something very interesting to check on the straps of his rucksack.

"Sam's right," Peter said. "It's clearly mentioned in the brochure that even though we're on the edge of the Northumberland National Park, we're actually on Ministry of Defence land. That's why we had to open those two gates to get in. Access to this area of the park is strictly limited. They don't want any Tom, Dick or Harriet wandering along and potentially blowing themselves up, so only people with a thorough knowledge of the area are allowed here." He smiled. "As it happens, I've been leading guided hikes and walks here for years and there's never been an issue."

"Never?" asked Martin.

"Not one. I can assure you all it's perfectly safe but, obviously, if any of you want to return to the hotel with Ross then you're more than welcome to."

There was some quiet conversation for a moment or two but nobody moved to get back on the minibus. Peter gave a relieved smile.

"Excellent," he said and pulled on his rucksack. "So we're now in a National Park that covers more than four hundred square miles, which is about a quarter of the county of Northumberland. It runs as far north as Hadrian's Wall and quite astonishingly, to my mind, it's apparently one of the least-visited National Parks in the country."

"Probably because people are worried about getting blown up," said Tony and Martin laughed.

Peter chuckled along with them. "There are very specific and clearly marked areas on the moor that have been used for live ammunition practice in the past but I can assure you our hike will take you nowhere near them."

"Is the whole area MoD ground?" Jo asked.

"Not quite but they do own a goodly amount and it's collectively known as the Otterburn Training Area. Some areas are off-limits or limited access, but I have full permission because I'm a certified guide to the area and have spent a lot of time around Irchester Flow." Peter looked at each of them in turn. "So, is everyone comfortable enough to continue?"

"I am," Jo said.

Sam nodded and Tony rubbed the corners of his mouth and looked at Martin. "I suppose so," he said.

"I should have paid more attention to the brochure," Martin said and reached out to touch Jo's hand.

"If everyone else is happy, then I am," said Gayle. She touched the bead on her worry bracelet.

"Excellent," said Ross and slammed the side door shut. "I'll see you back at the hotel then, folks. Have a good time."

Peter watched him reverse out of the parking space then clapped his hands to get the group's attention. "Okay then, folks. The hike is a total of about twelve miles, give or take and a lot of that is uphill." He chuckled. "And the bits that aren't will feel like it."

Jo and Sam laughed.

"The views, though, will more than make up for it, especially Irchester Flow when you see it."

"Well, I'm looking forward to it," said Sam. He took a GoPro camera out of his rucksack and fitted it to a pistol grip tripod.

"What's that?" asked Tony.

"A GoPro Hero. It's a multisports HD camera and pretty much indestructible."

"Are you making a film or something?" Martin asked.

"Kind of and I need to ask your permission. I won't be filming you directly, I'll be concentrating more on Gayle and the views, but you might appear. Would that be alright?"

"Do we get paid?" asked Tony.

"No, I'm afraid not."

"If you're filming Gayle," Tony said, "can we at least get to watch the out-takes?"

Martin smiled at his remark then looked at Jo and his smile soured as she scowled at him.

"It's for my YouTube channel and some of it will go on Gayle's Instagram account."

"I'm okay with you filming," said Jo and the others quickly agreed.

Tony soured the moment by adding, "I'll follow your Instagram account, if you like," but Gayle ignored him.

Sam switched the camera on and panned around the car park.

Peter gestured in the direction of the mound and rock formation. "My plan is that we'll head to the Devil's Steps first. It's a fairly brisk couple of miles so shouldn't be too taxing on any of us. Just please watch where you step. Most of the ground is solid and flat but you'll come across the occasional hillock or tuft and it's easy to turn an ankle."

"What happens if we do that?" asked Jo.

"Then you'll be in a lot of pain and we'll have to stop. I have a satellite phone for emergency use and if anything untoward does happen we can call in the mountain rescue team."

"How likely is it for anything untoward to happen?" Martin asked.

"Extremely unlikely. The hike will probably make you ache but it's very safe. We'll have a pleasant night on Irchester Flow then tomorrow morning we'll call in at a farm a friend of mine owns where we can have some egg sandwiches that'll be the best you've ever tasted."

"I thought you said this area was restricted?" Tony asked.

"It is," Peter said. "Why?"

"So who's that?"

Everyone turned to Tony. Jo saw he was looking up the hill past the mound.

"Who?" Peter asked.

"There," Tony pointed. "He's just at the top of the mound."

Jo shielded her eyes but couldn't see any movement at all.

"I can't see anyone," Peter said.

"I can't see him now but he was there," Tony insisted. "It was like a flash of movement, you know? I looked and I saw a man who looked like he had a bald head."

Jo felt like someone had tipped ice water on her.

"Are you okay?" Martin asked. "You look like you've seen a ghost."

"I'm fine," she said and hoped the words didn't sound as fake to him as they did to her.

Chapter 5

Jo, Five Weeks Ago

Jo sat in her car outside Hadlington Swimming Pool and looked up at the building in the fading light. It was all glass and steel and the exposed beams and supports made her think of some giant insect that was going to uproot itself and walk away.

Tonight was her first session with the over-forties swimming club and she was looking forward to it. She missed exercising and, since Olivia had left for Exeter, Jo had lost her badminton partner. Martin didn't enjoy the game and she didn't want to join the local club so she had stopped playing unless Olivia happened to be home. Meanwhile, she'd tried to find another activity to fill the time.

Martin's job meant he worked occasionally erratic and often long hours and the house began to feel lonely with just her rattling around in it. She tried a Pilates class at the Methodist church but didn't really enjoy it and then overheard her colleague Carole talking about the new swimming club she'd joined. Jo had swum a lot at college but, other than helping teach Olivia to swim, she hadn't done much since. The group, as Carole explained, was specifically for the older swimmer and Jo liked the idea of being able to swim a length in peace without kids doggy-paddling across her path.

She also wanted the distraction because there was a shift in the situation at home since Olivia had left. It sometimes felt like they were each trapped behind glass, able to see one another clearly but not quite interact. She didn't like that and because it was her natural inclination to worry, that just made the situation worse, even if he assured her it was normal to feel discombobulated.

This was all a period of big changes and, as he said, so long as they loved one another they'd manage. She agreed but decided that getting a few endorphin rushes might make that change a little easier to bear.

Carole walked across the car park, spotted Jo and waved wildly. Jo returned the wave and got out.

"I'm so glad you came," Carole said. She had bright red curly hair that seemed to ignite where the sun caught it. "Are you looking forward to it?"

"I think so."

"Oh, don't be worried. I was when I started. Bricking it, I was, but so long as you can swim, you'll be fine."

"I can swim, Carole."

"Then you're golden. Come on, I'll show you the ropes."

* * *

Jo got changed in a cubicle near the lockers and as she was putting her street clothes into her rucksack, she pressed her thumb on the underside of her wedding ring. She'd lost a bit of weight recently and now it wasn't as tight a fit as it had once been. She slipped it off and felt oddly bare but knew that was better than losing it in the pool as her finger shrank in the cool water. She slipped the ring into her trainer then went out into the general area. Carole was just putting her bag into a locker.

"My biggest fear on that first day," she said as Jo took the next locker over, "was that I'd slip on a wet tile and everyone would laugh at me."

"If you slip and anyone laughs, I'll thump them," said Jo firmly.

"I've always liked you," Carole said and laughed.

They walked through the foot bath and into the main complex. The smell of chlorine was strong and there was a faint mist in the air. The pool was set out into half a dozen lanes and swimmers were making their way up and down steadily.

"You can go in any lane," Carole explained, "but the ones in the middle tend to be the more serious swimmers. I usually go on the outer ones so I can grab onto the side if I need to. I'm not that quick or that strong."

"I used to be pretty competent," Jo said and sat on the edge of the pool. The water was chilly on her legs. "But it's been a while and even then, I was mostly floating around making sure Olivia was safe."

"I went a lot when my kids were small but then gave up." Carole sat next to her. "Bloody hell, the water's a bit nippy." She splashed some gently against her upper legs.

"You'll be fine," said Jo. She lowered herself into the water and the cold made her gasp. She let herself go under then surfaced and pushed her hair back from her eyes.

"You're a masochist," said Carole.

"It's only painful for a moment if you do it like that," said Jo.

"Easy for you to say, you're in now." Carole splashed more water on her legs. "Enjoy your swim. I'll catch you for a coffee after."

"Looking forward to it." Jo swam under a couple of lane markers until she was in the middle of the pool then dipped her head under and pushed off the side. She settled into a steady breaststroke and gradually picked up the pace until she was breathing a little more heavily.

There was a man in the next lane over whose pace was almost synchronised to hers so they seemed to pass one another under the overhead timing clock. He was bald with a tidy dark beard and his eyes were very blue. After the fourth time he raised a hand in greeting and she did the same.

* * *

Carole was waiting for Jo when she walked out of the changing rooms. Jo hadn't put her ring back on because, as she'd anticipated, the cool water had shrunk her finger too much.

"So how did it go?" Carole asked.

"I loved it," Jo said, still enjoying the endorphin rush. Her arm and leg muscles tingled with the exertion and she liked the feeling.

"So you'll be coming back?"

"Absolutely."

The coffee shop was at the far end of the foyer and formed by belt barriers with a counter at one end.

"As it's your first week I'll buy the drinks," Carole said. "What did you want?"

"I'll have an Americano," said Jo.

"Coming up. Grab us a seat."

Jo found a table near to the windows overlooking the pool. It didn't take Carole long to get served and she put the paper cups on the table. They talked as they drank and had almost finished their coffees when Jo noticed the bald swimmer with striking eyes. He sat on his own at a table on the other side of the enclosure. He was concentrating on his phone and his dress shirt and dark trousers suggested he'd come straight from work.

"I'd better be going," said Carole. "I'm famished and need to make dinner."

Jo checked her watch. It was almost six o'clock. "Me too."

The swimmer came by their table then and fixed them both with a wide smile. "I hope you enjoyed your swim today, ladies."

"Very much so," said Carole. "Did you?"

"I did," he said and looked at Jo for a moment too long. "I hope to see you next week."

Carole watched him walk away. "I think he liked you," she said.

"I'm a bit old for him," Jo said. "He can only be in his mid-thirties."

"I wouldn't complain," Carole said as she stood up. "He has lovely eyes."

Chapter 6

Jo took a couple of steadying breaths, exhaled slowly and touched the string on her wrist. To her surprise, it made her feel slightly better.

She hadn't seen anyone on the mound and it didn't seem as though anyone else had, other than Tony. He might have been confused, of course, and it was probably too far to know for sure if the mystery person was bald, or simply wearing a hat or climbing helmet. Either way, she tried to convince herself, there was no reason for her to worry.

"If the person you saw climbed over Black Shuck Hill, Tony, then he doesn't know the area. We'll talk to him when we catch up." Peter tightened the straps on his rucksack. "Let's go."

After everyone had put on their own packs and adjusted the straps for comfort, Peter led them across the gravel strip and over a stile.

"Why is it called Black Shuck Hill?" Sam filmed himself asking the question then turned the camera to Peter.

"There are plenty of legends surrounding the mound and the Devil's Steps. Back in the Middle Ages there was a land dispute and the lord of the manor brought in some mercenaries to defend the hill. He was a cruel man and the local villagers were apparently sick to death of him so they banded together to fight back. It was a terrible and bloody battle that took a lot of lives, and those people were buried on the field."

"You mean that mound is a mass grave?" asked Gayle.

"That can't be right," said Martin.

"Maybe," said Peter with a smile. "Even if it's not, you have to admit the legend sounds more exciting than saying it's just a lump on a hill."

He laughed and began to walk. Sam followed and held the GoPro above his head on the tripod as Gayle walked beside him. Tony fell into step behind them and Jo wondered if he was leching over Gayle's backside.

"Are you okay?" Martin asked.

"I'm fine," she said. "Are you worried about walking over a burial mound?"

He laughed. "Hardly." He took her hand and they started to walk. "I'm with my wife on a hike and we've got a weekend in a luxury hotel to look forward to. What more could I want?"

It sounded so much like the Martin before he took this latest job that she felt a flash of warmth across her chest. Maybe this weekend was just what they needed to get themselves back on track.

"How about the camping?" he asked. "Have you warmed to that, yet?"

"Not really, though I'm willing to put up with a night under canvas for a weekend of pampering, I have to say."

"How many massages are you planning to have?"

"At least two from the professionals on site and a couple of my husband's wonderful foot massages wouldn't go amiss either."

"Is it worth the hike to get a massage from me?"

"I'd walk for days to get one," she said and he laughed. "The hike'll be good fun, anyway. I'm looking forward to it and the people seem nice."

"I thought so, too. I was worried when I booked that we'd end up with a bunch of twats but, apart from lanky lad, they seem okay."

"He seems alright," she said. "I'm not so keen on Tony, though."

"Why?"

His surprise surprised her. Hadn't he been listening to the man? "I don't know, other than he gives me the creeps."

"The creeps? Why? Has he said anything to you?"

"Not to me, no, but he's been leering at Gayle."

"Really? Maybe that's just the way he is. You've only just met the bloke."

"So have you. Why are you defending him?"

"I'm not defending him, I'm just pointing out this is your first impression of him. Unless you've remembered where you know him from?"

"I don't think I know him, I just thought he looked familiar."

"Well, I haven't heard him say anything out of the ordinary and you know what I'm like when blokes are leering at young women. If I heard him say anything, I'd pick him up on it." He squeezed her hand. "I don't want us to fight, Jo."

"We're not," she said, hurt by his inference that if they were, it was her fault. "I'm just pointing it out."

"I know, I'm sorry." His voice cracked. "So much has happened recently and I want to put it behind us and move forward. I want this weekend to work for us both. We need a chance to clear our heads and clear the ways." He pulled her to him and kissed her.

She put her hand on his chest and kissed him back. "I want the same thing," she said.

"That's good."

Jo saw the others were quite a distance further up the hill. "We ought to get moving. We're like the naughty kids straggling behind."

They held hands. "Where did you get that?" he asked, gesturing at her bracelet.

"Gayle gave it to me in the minibus. She makes them and sells them on Etsy."

"People buy those things?"

"Don't be horrible," she said with mock indignation. "It's nice."

"It's a bit of string with a bead on it. I think Olivia stopped making them when she was about ten."

"It's a stress bracelet," she corrected him.

"Does it stress you out that you paid for a bit of string?"

"Leave it alone," she said but couldn't help smiling. "It was nice of her to give it to me."

"So what does it do?"

"It's a focus for mindfulness. I suppose you use it like a rosary and stroke it when you're feeling a bit overwhelmed."

"I'd be overwhelmed if I'd bought that without realizing how basic it was."

"You wouldn't know stress if it bit you on the arse, Martin Harper."

He laughed. "Oh, I'm sure I would."

They began to walk in easy silence and she kept an eye on the ground because she didn't want to be the one who went over with a twisted ankle. After a while he stopped to take a photograph and waved her on. Keen to push herself a little, she lengthened her stride and picked up her pace. By the time she caught up with Peter, Tony had drifted off to the right while Sam filmed Gayle talking to the camera off to the left.

"How are you?" Peter asked as she fell into step beside him.

"Doing okay," Jo said, catching her breath. The incline of the hill was greater than she'd expected and she could feel a slight burn in her calves.

"The hills can take it out of you," he said. "Do you walk much?"

"I do and I swim each week too."

"That's marvellous exercise."

"What about you?" she asked.

"I do a couple of these hikes a week. I used to do more but in reality, I'm not quite the spring chicken I am in my head."

"Have you been doing this for long?"

"A good few years now, Mrs Harper."

"Please," she said, "call me Jo."

"Thank you."

"So how did you get into it?"

"I'm a local lad and I've always loved the area and spent as much time in it as I possibly could. When our kids left home and I got made redundant, I took a chance when a position for a tour company opened up. I'll be honest, it's one of the best things I ever did and it gives me access to places I wasn't able to go before. I'm a fell-runner and some of the MoD land is perfect."

"So does your wife run, too?"

"No. She used to like walking and would sometimes come on the tours with me, but she thought people running up a mountain needed their heads testing." He laughed. "Maybe she was right."

"Didn't she want to come along this time?"

"She couldn't. She passed away a couple of years ago."

He said it in such a matter-of-fact manner that it took her a moment to properly process what he'd said. She looked at him and he looked at her. "I'm so sorry," she said.

"Don't be. She enjoyed life to the full and we had a good time together. Unfortunately, I'm at the age now where my friends and loved ones are moving on." He gave her a sad smile. "Anyway, enough about that. Did I hear you say you had a daughter who's just left for university?"

"That's right." Jo glanced over her shoulder and saw Martin and Tony were walking together and talking.

"I remember those days," said Peter. "We were overjoyed to get the freedom but then really missed the kids as they got on with their lives."

"Yes, I think we're both struggling with that."

"It'll get better," he said.

"Really?"

He gave a quick look. "Nope, but sometimes it doesn't hurt to tell a little white lie." He smiled and touched her arm. "You'll be fine."

Chapter 7

The hill ended at a small ridge. Beyond it was a wide footpath that ran along the base of Black Shuck Hill, which loomed over Jo now.

The mound was covered with thick grass. Patches of heather grew amongst the lumps of rock that poked out at various points. From this angle, it looked impossible to climb up onto.

Jo followed Peter onto the footpath then stepped to one side to let Gayle up. The younger woman lost her footing and slipped back. She threw up an arm for support and Jo grabbed her and pulled her up.

"Wow," Gayle said. "You've got some strong arms there."

"It's because of the swimming. I think my upper body strength is the best it's ever been."

"You might need it," said Gayle and looked up at the mound. She turned to Peter and raised her eyebrows. "I don't see how we're going to be able to climb up that."

"We won't," said Peter. "Black Shuck Hill is a glorious piece of scenery but it's basically inaccessible from here. If you want to get onto it, you follow the footpath along for the best part of a mile then there are a series of switchbacks to get to the top. Instead, we're going up the Devil's Steps."

"Which doesn't sound much easier," said Jo.

"The name is deceptive," Peter said with a smile. "Come on." He led the group a hundred yards or so to the right until they reached the huge slab of rock that slanted at forty-five degrees.

"The Devil's Steps," Peter said, with a ta-dah hand gesture.

"That doesn't look a lot better," said Martin.

"Oh, it is," said Peter. "The accepted wisdom is that at one point, this was one long mound. Then part of it sheered off and the top bit slid down into the valley."

"I'll bet that was spectacular," said Sam.

"Noisy too," agreed Peter. "You certainly wouldn't have wanted to be standing in the bowl of the valley when it went."

"So why is it called the Devil's Steps?" Gayle asked.

"Because of all the pits and crevasses." Peter gestured towards a few of them. "The angle means it's very difficult to come down this way but if you're going uphill, as we are, they effectively make up a series of steps. It's more difficult to navigate the closer you are to Black Shuck but the eastern edge has its own issues too." He moved along the bottom of the rock face and the group followed him. "When the mound broke it sheared off one side and created that hill of scree."

"What's scree?" asked Sam.

"It's a deep mass of loose stones and although it doesn't look like much it can be treacherous underfoot. The stones can shift and take you with them, or you can get your feet caught and then you're talking broken bones."

"Best to avoid it then," said Sam.

"I'd say so, Lanky Lad," agreed Tony.

"You're right," said Peter. "If you do end up on scree for some reason, the best bet is to try and turn sideways and lean your weight on your back foot. Stopping's the issue, you see, and this section has the added danger of a sharp drop at the bottom."

They all peered over the scree slope. Twenty or thirty feet down there was a kind of crater with a thick ridge around it. Jo couldn't see the ground beyond it.

"How far is that drop?" she asked.

"About a hundred foot or so. The big danger is that you get carried down to the crater by the scree and gravity does the rest to pop you over the edge."

"Ouch," said Martin.

"This feels a bit dangerous," said Sam and sounded worried.

"Everything's dangerous," said Peter. "But this is as safe as houses so long as we're careful."

Jo looked at Martin and he raised his eyebrows in response but didn't say anything.

Peter walked along the footpath to a small set of steps that had been built with rocks at the edge of the slab face. "Of course, there's nothing to say we can't walk around Black Shuck if anyone's worried about going this way."

"How long would that take?" asked Tony.

"A few hours," said Peter. "Anyone fancy it?" He looked around the group but nobody volunteered. "Okay then, we'll set off. Does anyone want to go on the mound side where it's a bit more difficult?"

"I fancy the challenge," said Martin.

"Me too," said Sam. "I can then film Gayle and it'll be a more exciting background."

Martin gave him a glance as if that was the weirdest reason he'd ever heard, then caught Jo's eye and smiled.

"I'm going on the easier side," said Gayle. "The grip on these boots isn't the best ever."

"Same here," said Tony, though Jo wondered what he'd have said if Gayle had made a different choice.

His decision helped make hers, too. "I'll go up with Gayle," she said.

"Follow me then," said Peter and he led the way up the steps onto the slab.

They gathered on a narrow ledge about three feet wide. From there, Jo could see the holes that provided the steps more clearly. From this angle they looked relatively evenly placed and not too deep.

"It's as simple as climbing some stairs," Peter said, "just a bit steeper. Keep your eye on the ground to make sure the footing is where you think it's going to be and, for those on the eastern side, keep well away from the edge."

"Remember the scree," Jo said to Martin and gave him the thumbs up. He returned the gesture.

The group separated and Martin worked his way carefully along the slab until he was almost at Black Shuck. Sam followed in his footsteps. Peter took a route up the middle and Tony went behind him, just off to the right.

"Are you ready?" Jo asked.

"No." Gayle smiled nervously. "But I don't want to get left behind."

"I won't leave you behind," Jo said and walked over towards the eastern side but kept a gap of more than ten feet between her and the edge. Gayle walked to her right and Jo resisted the urge to tell her to be careful.

The holes seemed well spaced here but she kept her eye on the ground to make sure she didn't miss a step. Every now and again she looked off to her right at the spectacular view that opened up. Now that it wasn't obscured by the mound or rock, she could see the trees at the top of the valley. The sky above was a deep blue and there were few clouds. To her right, beyond the scree and crater, the hill wound its way down. Bracken and bushes spotted the rolling hillsides in shades of greens and browns and a stream cut through the base. Some dry-stone walls marked out a patchwork but most of the area was open. As the valley wound further on, she could see a dense forest that climbed up one of the valley sides.

"This is a good workout for your calves and thighs," said Gayle, slightly out of breath.

Jo agreed though she was enjoying the burn. "Better than swimming," she said. "And it's a better view than the pool too."

Gayle laughed. "Doing Zumba comes a poor second to this."

They walked in silence until they were about three quarters of the way up the slab. Jo could feel the exertion in her core by then and her breath was hot in her chest.

She heard a scuffing and the sounds of stones sliding to her left. When she looked, she saw Tony had fallen to one knee. He didn't look happy.

"Are you okay?" she asked.

"Do I look it?"

'Charming,' she thought. "Not really."

He shook his head then apparently saw the funny side because he laughed. "Hey, it could be worse."

"Just take it steady." Gayle had moved ahead now and seemed to be getting closer to the edge. "Hey," Jo called. "Be careful."

"I'm fine," Gayle assured her.

Jo set off behind her and had only gone a few feet when she heard a rush of footsteps and ragged breathing. She looked to her left and saw Tony coming at her quickly. His arms were outstretched and he had a horribly blank look on his face.

"I'm falling!" he shouted but it looked like he was running.

There wasn't time to move out of the way, so she braced herself. He hit her hard, one hand on her upper arm, the other on her side. The impact knocked her sideways and she staggered to keep her balance. Her foot came down on a hole and she began to tip back. She tried to twist around to see where the edge of the slab was and then Gayle was right in front of her. The young woman's mouth was a perfect 'O' of surprise as Jo bumped into her and then both women were falling towards the edge.

Chapter 8

Jo tried to push Gayle to one side but couldn't get a proper grip and then she was falling.

Gayle screamed and toppled back and then dropped out of sight.

Jo landed hard, but quickly got onto all fours and crawled to the edge, terrified of what she might see. She heard the slap of boots on stone and then Peter was standing beside her.

"Gayle!" he shouted. "Stay still."

"I can't!"

Gayle was sitting in the scree but sliding towards the crater. She looked terrified. Jo quickly got to her feet.

"What can we do?" she asked.

"I'll get her." Peter ran up the slab a few feet and then jumped off the side. He landed on the scree with a heavy crunch and managed to keep to his feet even as the stones shifted beneath him. He turned sideways and moved in Gayle's direction. She tried to scramble back to him but the scree was moving freely under her now.

"Try to stay still!" Peter shouted.

"Holy fuck, he jumped!" Sam exclaimed. He was standing on the other side of Jo now.

Martin came up behind her and put his hand on her shoulder.

Peter slid and stepped through the scree at a good pace. The noise of the shifting stones grew louder all the time. Gayle screamed and her eyes were wide and searching but she'd stopped trying to move. When he was close enough, he reached for her. She grabbed for his hand but the action rocked her backwards. He went past her then turned and came back, running against the flow like someone racing up a down escalator. He made ground and grabbed her under the arms so she could get to her feet.

Jo gasped and Martin gripped her shoulder. She wanted to do something to help but didn't know what.

"Just run!" Peter shouted and then they were both racing up the hill, moving quickly enough that the stones sliding against them weren't a problem.

Martin and Sam were transfixed by the action.

"Help me!" Gayle shouted.

Jo quickly lay on the slab and pushed herself forward until she was leaning over the edge. She held out her hand.

"Grab on!" she shouted.

Gayle took a bigger stride and Peter gave her a shove. Jo's fingers closed around Gayle's wrist and she gripped hard but fell forward. Jo gritted her teeth as her arm was wrenched but held on tight. Martin lay beside her and reached for Gayle's other hand.

"I have her," he shouted.

"Pull back," Jo said. It was difficult to get any leverage but they managed to pull Gayle towards them enough that she was close to the edge. Peter was right behind her now and bent forward to grab the back of her thighs. He pushed her up and Jo and Martin pulled hard at the same time. Gayle came up over the edge of the slab and they let go of her as she collapsed in a heap.

Peter ran to the edge and Martin reached for him but missed. Jo grabbed his wrist and Peter did the rest, pulling himself up onto the slab and rolling away from Gayle. He got quickly to his feet and shook out his hands then helped Jo up.

"Thank you," he said.

Sam squatted next to Gayle but she knocked his concerned hands away. "I'm fine," she said.

Satisfied that Gayle was safe, Jo spun on her heel and let her anger soar. Tony stood a few feet away rubbing his hands on his trousers. There was a rip in one knee and she could see blood.

"What the fuck do you think you were doing, you twat?" she demanded as she strode towards him.

He held up his hands. His palms were scuffed and bloody. "I'm sorry, Jo, I slipped. I was moving too fast and didn't check my footing and went over. It wasn't my fault."

"Of course it was your fault," she said. Her throat felt hot and tight with anger. "You knocked me sideways because you were running at me. If Peter hadn't been here, then…"

"But I was," Peter said gently, stepping between her and Tony.

"It was an accident," said Martin, coming around the other side of her. "I saw it."

"He came at me like a bloody train," Jo said, determined not to be silenced.

"He fell," said Peter.

The fact that both Peter and Martin were trying to calm things down just made her angrier. "I'm the one he hit hard enough to push me into Gayle. You don't get that momentum from tripping, do you? If Gayle had been closer to the side, perhaps Peter wouldn't have been able to catch her."

"But I did," said Peter calmly. "I know you're angry, Jo, and I understand it, but we're all safe."

Tony continued to watch her with curiously dead eyes and no contrition in his expression. She glanced at Peter, who glared at Tony but didn't say anything. Jo didn't dare look at Martin because if he was doing his 'I'm concerned' face after failing to back her up then she would properly blow up at him.

Nobody said anything and all Jo could hear was her own roaring blood and Martin's heavy breathing. She stroked the string bracelet then turned away from Tony with disgust. She leaned over Gayle. "How are you?"

"Just a bit shook up, that's all," she said and sat up. Sam knelt beside her but she pushed him away. "Leave me alone, alright?"

"What did I do?" he asked.

"Nothing," she said coldly.

"I'm sorry," he said.

"Yeah," she muttered.

"You're safe," Jo said and the knowledge seemed to take the edge off her anger a little. She looked back at Tony and flexed her fingers, trying to push the aggression out. He held up his hands and she took a few deep breaths, in through the nose and out through the mouth. Had she made a mistake in the heat of the moment?

Peter knelt beside Tony and took a small white pack out of his rucksack. "I have basic first aid here," he said. "Let me look at those hands, Tony."

Martin touched Jo's arm. "Are you okay?"

"Not really," she said but her anger was fading now.

"Well, for what it's worth, I think you reacted well. Better than me and Sam. You saved Gayle."

"And so did Peter," she said.

Peter got to his feet and stowed the first aid kit back into his rucksack. "We both did."

"I couldn't believe it when you jumped onto the scree," Martin said. "That stuff's lethal but you were all over it like a mountain goat."

"I used to run on it, but my legs aren't really up to that task any more. I used to find the idea of running over an ever-shifting surface very exhilarating, where a moment's miscalculation could break your leg."

"I'm not sure I'd call it exhilarating," said Gayle and that made Peter laugh. She smiled at his reaction and got to her feet. "It was close, wasn't it? Thank you for what you did, Peter. You too, Jo."

"All's well that ends well," Peter said. He looked at Gayle then Jo and both of them gave him nods. "Now if everyone's okay, I think it's probably best if we move on."

Chapter 9

Jo, Three Weeks Ago

On her third session at the over-forties swimming club, Jo pushed herself hard and enjoyed the exertion as she got into the rhythm. When she got out of the changing room, she found the coffee shop enclosure almost full of parents talking, checking their phones or looking out over the pool. There were children everywhere.

Jo got the drinks while Carole found them a table.

"Inter-schools water polo," Carole said when Jo sat down. "It's a bit noisy, isn't it? I come here to get away from the kids."

"If this happens again we'll have to find another coffee shop."

"Couldn't agree more," said Carole. Her expression brightened as she looked over Jo's shoulder. "It looks like our friend with the incredible eyes is trying to find somewhere to sit."

Jo turned in her chair. He was standing at the counter holding a cup of coffee and surveying the enclosure. He looked like he was about to give up and leave. They'd fallen into sync again during the session and acknowledged one another as they passed.

"Shall we ask him to join us?" Carole asked.

She seemed eager and Jo didn't want to let her down. "That's a good idea."

Carole waved him over and when he got to the table he stood behind the spare chair. He wore a suit without a tie and the light caught the water droplets he hadn't dried off his bald head. "Evening, ladies. It's busy today."

"We were just saying that," said Carole and gave him a big smile. "That's why we thought you might like to join us. You don't have to worry, we won't bite."

He sat down and put his coffee on the table then slid his bag under the chair. "I'm sure you won't." He held out his hand to Carole. "I'm Tim Robson."

"Carole Bridges," she said as they shook hands.

"And you are?" he asked and shook Jo's hand. She saw him look at her fingers.

"Jo Harper."

"Nice to meet you both," he said. "You know, I've been coming here for a couple of months and apart from the occasional wave, you're the first people who've been properly friendly to me and it's nice. Not that I joined to meet people or anything, but it's always good to exchange a smile and a hello, isn't it?"

"I'd say so," said Carole. "So, what made you come along?"

"Fitness," he said. "I played a lot of squash then broke my ankle, which made me really grumpy. I was moping around the house and my wife suggested I come swimming."

Carole seemed ever so slightly deflated to hear he was married. "Best exercise," she said. "I read about it on

Mumsnet. Plus I'm not the right size for yoga class." She touched her stomach. "It'd take me the whole session to get into downward dog while all those stick-thin ladies were tying themselves in knots." She seemed pleased to draw laughter from both Jo and Tim.

"How about you, Jo?" he asked.

"Exercise for me, too. I played badminton a lot but with Olivia away at uni, I haven't got anyone to play with."

"That's a shame," he said with a slight smile that she couldn't properly read.

"Do you have children, Tim?" Carole asked.

"Not yet," he said. "We're still at the 'enjoying trying' stage."

Carole rested her chin in her hand. "Not been married long then?"

"A little over a year."

Carole seemed happy to lead the conversation so Jo left her to it. In this light, Tim looked even younger than she'd first supposed.

"So neither of you ladies are married then?"

"I am," said Jo.

"Are you?" Tim sounded surprised enough that Jo glanced at him and he looked abashed. "I'm sorry, I don't know why I said it like that. It's just that you aren't wearing a ring."

Jo looked at her bare finger. "I take it off in the water because I've lost some weight and it's a bit loose. I don't want to lose it in the pool."

"That makes sense," Tim said. "I honestly didn't mean anything when I sounded so surprised."

"Don't worry about it," she said.

"You and Martin have been together for a while, haven't you?" Carole asked. "Ten years or more, isn't it?"

"That's right."

"And do you just have the one child?" Tim asked.

"We're empty nesters," she said. "It's taking a bit of getting used to."

"I can imagine." Tim finished his coffee and checked his watch. "I'd best be off. The old ball-and-chain will be texting me soon to find out why I'm not home for dinner." He smiled disarmingly and got up. "I hope to see you both next week," he said and left.

"I like him," said Carole as she watched him go.

"Really?" Jo asked. "You hid it well."

Carole feigned surprise. "He's very charming. His wife is a lucky lady." She sipped her coffee. "I hope I didn't seem desperate."

"I was only kidding," Jo said, concerned she'd hurt her friend's feelings.

"It's just that these days, with looking after the kids, I only come into contact with new men on dating apps and I've never had much success on them." She watched as Tim walked out of the building. "Window shopping's not bad, is it?"

"Not at all," said Jo. "Not at all."

Chapter 10

Tony kept well ahead of both Jo and Gayle as they made their way up the remainder of the slab.

Sam reached the top first then climbed up onto Black Shuck Hill and took some photographs with his phone. "What a view," he said.

The group made their way over to him and Jo was happy to stand on a flat grassy surface that felt like she wouldn't slip on it.

"Wow," said Gayle.

"Come over here," said Sam. "Let me get a couple of pictures of you for your channel."

Jo thought for a moment she wasn't going to move but then Gayle nodded and walked over to him. He said something quietly and she shook her head but gave him a quick smile.

Martin put his arm over Jo's shoulder. "How're you feeling now?"

"A bit better."

"Calmed down a bit?"

"Not really. Tony didn't trip, Martin. He came at me." She couldn't get the image of him barrelling towards her out of her head.

"But why would he do that?"

She could tell he was trying to be level-headed about it but that wasn't what she wanted now. She knew what she'd seen and the jolt of impact wasn't of someone losing their balance.

"I don't know, but that doesn't mean he didn't do it."

"We don't even know him."

"I told you I thought he looked familiar."

"Jo, there's a big difference between someone looking familiar and knowing you enough to want to hurt you." It sounded so sensible but she couldn't accept it. "And he did fall, because he bashed himself up in the process, didn't he?"

"Serves him right."

Martin barked a quick laugh. "If you're so sure, do you want me to ask him?"

"Oh yeah," she said sarcastically, "great idea. How exactly do you go about asking a man outright if he meant to knock your wife over into a scree pile?"

He chuckled softly. "It might make the rest of the hike a little uncomfortable."

"Yeah, just a little bit."

"But I will ask him and not be stupid about it. How does that sound?"

"That sounds okay."

She wanted him to pull her into a hug but, instead, he stepped back and took out his phone to take a picture of the view. "I want you to enjoy this weekend, Jo. I want us" – he emphasised the word – "to enjoy it. We can make this work."

"I know," she said.

* * *

Some of the party groaned when they saw how steep the hill was up to the ridge, but Jo began walking without complaint because she thought the exercise might take her mind off the incident on the Devil's Steps.

Martin kept up with her for a while and then dropped back but that was fine for the moment. As much as she was enjoying their closeness, there was something almost magical about being on the side of a valley and walking alone. She took deep breaths of fresh air filled with the scents of moss and heather.

The peaks and valleys to her left and right made her feel part of something much bigger than herself and she looked towards the trees ahead, now silhouetted against a sky starting to fill with cloud. When she turned to look back at where the minibus dropped them it seemed a long way away, barely visible over the rise of Black Shuck Hill.

Peter wasn't too far behind her. Martin was further back and talking intently with Tony. It made her feel a little uncomfortable and not just because there was something about Tony she couldn't quite put her finger on. It clung to the back of her mind like a snagged nail, but she couldn't quite bring it into focus.

Gayle and Sam were even further back and he was holding up his phone as they walked.

Jo waited for Peter to reach her and fell into step with him.

"You're coping better with the hill than some of the others," he said. "How are you feeling now?"

"I'm getting there."

"Good. A little calmer, I hope?"

She laughed. "I take it by calmer you mean do I still want to rip Tony's head off?"

He laughed too. "That's what I was thinking."

"In that case, I'm not quite calm, then."

"My wife always used to say that nobody, in the history of being told to calm down, has ever calmed down."

"Your wife was a very wise lady."

"She liked to think so."

"Did you see Tony fall?" It wouldn't change things if Peter had or hadn't, but an objective viewpoint on the matter might let her better deal with it.

"I didn't but I must admit I'm curious as to why you think he didn't just fall. Did you know him before today?"

"No. I thought he looked familiar when we were introduced but I don't know him."

Peter nodded as if he'd guessed as much. He walked in silence for a few moments then cleared his throat. "I come into these hikes without knowing who's going to be on them and I've never met you or Tony before. I have nothing other than my first impressions, so you need to take what I'm going to say on that level."

"Okay."

"I've walked the Devil's Steps a lot and know the layout well and, even though I didn't see Tony fall, I can't square in my head how he could have done so and yet caught you in such a way to knock you over. The last time I looked you two weren't walking that close together."

"So what does that mean?"

"Maybe nothing," he said and shrugged. "In the end, nobody came to any real harm but if I were you, I'd perhaps keep an eye out."

"Keep an eye out?" The phrase produced a chilly little flutter across the back of her neck.

"I don't mean anything horrible," he said and touched her arm lightly as if to assure her. "My wife always said I had a melodramatic turn of phrase. I just meant that if he's clumsy, then perhaps you need to keep away from him. There are a lot of hills you wouldn't want to end up rolling down."

His advice was so prosaic that the chilly flutter dissipated. What had she expected him to say? That Tony was out to get her? Maybe she was just being paranoid. Maybe she needed Gayle's stress bracelet more than she'd thought.

"Good advice," she said. "Thank you."

"Oh I'm full of it," he said. "I really should take some of it to heart once in a while. Like not jumping off a cliff at my time of life."

"I think we're all like that."

"You may be right, Jo. I'm going to crack on, if that's okay?"

You go ahead," she said.

Peter walked away and Jo turned to look back down the hill again. Martin had left Tony behind and gave her a wave. She waited for him to catch up.

"Hey," he said. He was out of breath.

"I saw you talking with Tony."

"Uh-huh. I told him what he did was reckless and stupid and he agreed but says it was an accident."

"Peter thought it was, too."

"That seems to be the prevailing wisdom," he said. "Oh, and one other thing. Have you ever been to Cleethorpes?"

The question was so random it took her by surprise. "I don't think so. Why? Are we calling in there on our way home or something?"

"Hardly. I mentioned to Tony that you thought you recognised him–"

"Oh, Martin, please tell me you didn't."

"Why wouldn't I?" He seemed surprised. "I asked where he came from and he said Cleethorpes, born and bred. He's never heard of Hadlington and can't remember the last time he was in Northamptonshire, so it's unlikely you'd ever have met up. I think he reminds you of someone you've seen on television. Maybe he's a dead ringer for a photofit picture from Crimewatch that stuck in your head."

"I hope not."

"It'd be different though, wouldn't it? Going on a hiking trip with a serial killer?"

"That's not the kind of different I'd like."

"Thinking about it, I wouldn't either."

Jo slowed down and slipped off her rucksack. "I'm going to get a drink. You carry on and I'll catch up."

"You'll overtake me," he said and kept walking.

She took a couple of good swigs of her water then looked back towards Tony. He was keeping his distance from her and really leaning into the hill as if the angle was taking it out of his legs. She noticed he kept slipping on the grass and wondered if the tread of his boots was wearing down. If it was, that might explain his fall on the slab.

Tony caught her eye and raised his hand in a hesitant wave. She waved back. She looked ahead and saw Peter and Martin were walking together and very close to the treeline now.

Jo screwed the cap on her bottle and set off again.

Chapter 11

Jo took some photographs even though she knew they wouldn't capture the scale and majesty of the scenery. But they would at least give Olivia some idea of the views when she emailed her about the weekend.

Sam passed her with a nod and Jo waited for Gayle, who trudged slowly behind him.

"You aren't waiting for me, are you?"

"I was taking photos," Jo admitted. "But now you're here we might as well walk up together."

"Thanks. This has been harder than I thought."

"I think we're near the top of the valley now so you've got a nice downhill run to look forward to next."

"There's no way I'm running anywhere."

They walked on at a steady pace as Gayle got her breath back. Jo had assumed the trees on the ridge were part of a wood but now she could see it was little more than a copse. Peter and Martin were already picking their way through and Sam wasn't far behind them.

"Are you still angry with Tony?" Gayle asked.

"Kind of. Peter and Martin both said, in the nicest possible way, that I'd got the wrong end of the stick, but I can't quite let it go."

"You really should," Gayle said, "otherwise it'll eat you up. Can I show you a little trick I've learned?"

"If you want."

"Okay, take this bag off me." Gayle held up her hands and Jo looked at her with a frown. Gayle shook her hand. "Take it." Jo pretended to and felt just a little bit silly. "Now open the bag." Jo pantomimed doing so. "Now take your angry feelings for Tony." Gayle waved her fist and Jo matched the movement and felt a surge of aggression as she pressed her nails into her palm. "Can you feel that negativity?"

"I can."

"So then, drop it into the bag," Gayle said.

Jo held her clenched fist over the imaginary bag and then dropped it in. Suddenly it didn't feel so silly.

"Seal the bag," urged Gayle.

Jo pretended to tie the bag up.

"Now drop it at your feet and we walk away from it."

She did and felt a wave of relief.

"Does that feel a bit better?"

It hadn't worked completely but she did feel less stressed about Tony. "Yes, it did. Thank you."

"You're welcome. I was shown that when my anxiety really started to kick in and found it useful. I drop a lot of bags at my feet."

"And how do you feel after your little misadventure?"

"Well my bum hurts from all those stones and I'm dying inside from embarrassment. I had to bag up my annoyance and frustration with Sam otherwise I'd have killed him. If it hadn't been for you and Peter, I'd have slid into that crater and probably fallen over the edge. Sam just sat there like a spare part."

"Maybe he was in shock."

"Maybe," Gayle said. "But he should have helped and even though he kept apologising, it ate into me."

"I'm sure he was sorry."

"He was and that's kind of the problem." Gayle shook out her hands as if they were full of tension.

"What's wrong?"

"I thought I could ride it out, you know, but I can't." She took several deep breaths and let them out steadily then gave Jo a forced smile. "You don't want to hear this, do you? I met you an hour ago and you've already saved my life so I can't expect you to listen to my woes."

"Think about the lesson you just gave me," said Jo. It was more than that though. If Olivia were in a situation she needed to talk through, she'd want someone to give her stepdaughter the time of day to listen. "Talk to me."

"I need you to understand that I like Sam a lot. He's kind and funny and looks out for me but…"

"He thinks more of you than you do of him?"

"Precisely. He helped me through things at uni and I appreciated that when other friends cut me dead and…" She tapered off. "He said he loved me but understood I wasn't in the right place to respond, which was nice of him. He's never put pressure on me so when he suggested this hike I agreed because I thought if I focussed on us hard enough, I could push myself into loving him. Which is shit, really, and I'm sure he'd hate it if he knew."

"Have you slept together before?"

"Nope." Gayle's smile was shy. "But it was my idea to share a tent."

"You're not there though, are you?"

Gayle shook her head. "I wasn't sure but his reaction when I fell pretty much confirmed in my head we're not destined to be together."

"Have you told him?"

"Not yet. I just got onto him for not rescuing me."

They'd reached the trees. The others were working their way through and Sam's red trousers kept catching the light.

"What should I do?" Gayle asked.

"It's difficult for me to say," Jo said warily.

"What would you say to Olivia in the same position?"

"I'd tell her to do what made her feel comfortable, rather than try to please someone else. What's good for them perhaps isn't best for you."

"Yeah," Gayle said with the slightest nod of her head. "I think you're right."

The copse was barely more than a dozen feet deep and once under the canopy it was dark and quiet. Jo followed a natural path between the narrow trucks and the ground was covered with a thin layer of mulch that swallowed up the sound of their progress.

Gayle stumbled over some bramble and almost fell into a tree. She grabbed the trunk with both hands and grinned at Jo. "I'm the clumsiest person in the world."

"I don't think you're even the clumsiest person in our group."

Something snapped off to their right like a whipcrack. Jo looked towards where she assumed the sound had come from. The trees were thicker there with bramble growing against a couple of the trunks like a bush.

"What was that?" Gayle whispered.

"Maybe a branch fell off a tree."

"Perhaps it's a big cat," Gayle said. "There was a thing on the news a little while ago and I'm sure it was in Northumberland. Someone filmed a puma or something walking across a farmer's field."

"They're just hoaxes," Jo said.

"Or what about that bald man Tony said he saw?"

Jo felt a quick chill of fright across her shoulders. "The others would have seen him, surely?"

Another snap cut her off.

"Maybe not," said Gayle. "Should we run?"

The bramble rustled and Tony came through it. He was zipping up his fly and grinned when he saw them.

"Hello, ladies."

Jo let out her breath in a rush. "Jesus Christ."

"Not quite," said Tony. His grin got wider. "I didn't realise you ladies were waiting for me."

"We weren't," said Gayle sourly, as if the very idea was distasteful.

"You were certainly looking this way."

"We wondered what the noise was," Jo said.

"You listened to me peeing?" he asked.

Gayle said "Ew," and shook her head.

Jo smiled tightly at him. "If we'd known you were going, we'd have listened more intently."

Tony frowned as if he couldn't work out whether she was joking or not. After a moment, he said, "You're dirtier than you look, obviously."

"You'll never know," Jo said and walked away from him.

As they came out of the trees, Peter and Martin were deep in conversation a few feet away. Sam was off to the left, on slightly higher ground, holding his phone up and looking as if he'd lost a fiver and found ten pence. There were more grey clouds overhead now.

Jo had expected to see Irchester Flow but instead at least two miles of moorland spread out in front of her, running on a slight downhill gradient to another stand of trees. These were thicker though, almost a small wood, and stretched further east.

"It looks like the weather forecast was right," Peter was saying.

"Are we due much rain?" Martin asked.

"A few hours' worth," Peter said, "but it won't be until later on so we should be fine."

"How far is it until we get to the place?" Gayle asked.

"Two and a half miles to that wood and the Flow is just on the other side." Peter checked his watch. "We'll be there within three quarters of an hour which'll give us plenty of time to make camp and get some dinner."

Tony came out of the woods. "You weren't all waiting for me, were you?" No one said anything. "What's Lanky Lad doing?"

"Still trying to get a signal," said Martin.

"Why doesn't he just give up? He's starting to annoy me wandering around with his arm in the air."

"I hope he keeps doing it," muttered Jo.

Peter smiled at her. "Let's get going. The quicker we move, the quicker we eat."

Chapter 12

Peter led them into the small wood where the canopy was so dense, they were immediately plunged into twilight. The trail was easy to see and it didn't take long to reach the other side.

"Welcome to Irchester Flow," he said with a grand sweep of his arm.

Jo stepped onto a grassy plateau half the size of a football field. They were standing some way from the edge of what appeared to be a horseshoe shape of limestone cliffs and were high enough up that the ground below looked a long way away. Around the edge was a lip of flat limestone blocks that made a path of cracked rocks.

"Wow," said Jo.

"I know," Peter said. "Photographs just don't capture the majesty of it, do they?"

"It looks incredible," said Sam. He was already walking towards the edge with the GoPro raised above his head.

"From where we are," Peter said, "the Flow looks like a huge horseshoe that we're at the centre of. If you're at the bottom, which we unfortunately won't have time to get to on this hike, it looks almost like an amphitheatre and is really something to behold."

He walked towards the edge and beckoned for them to follow him. Martin took Jo's hand. She made sure there was plenty of space between her and Tony because the last place she wanted to be was anywhere near his apparent clumsiness.

"Why's it called Irchester Flow?" Gayle asked.

"That small depression you can see," he said and pointed it out, "used to be the site of a natural spring. The cavity would fill during heavy rain and run down a small channel to the lip of the cliff. The waterfall then dropped straight down and, by all accounts, was very spectacular."

"So what happened to it?" asked Martin.

"Nature," said Peter. "The spring found a lower outlet point near the base of the cliff and it still feeds a brook today that runs into the Breamish River a mile or so away."

"How big is the drop?" asked Sam.

"The cliff is pretty much a vertical face here and it's two hundred and sixty feet at the highest point."

"Wow," said Jo. "That's a big drop." As they moved closer to the edge she could see the sides were steep slopes that ran down to the basin. Mossy areas spotted the lower levels of rock and a few straggly trees grew out of gaps with their branches reaching for the sky.

"It is," Peter said. "Because the limestone is full of nooks and crannies, the army and mountain rescue service use the face for training purposes."

"Have you ever climbed it?" Martin asked.

"Not for a long time. I'm too old for it now."

They stopped by the path. "How close can we go?" Jo asked.

"As much as your balance and tolerance for heights will let you," said Peter. "We're all adults here and you don't need me prattling on about health and safety, but don't take any risks. This limestone path isn't actually the edge of the cliff but you should pretend it is. However, you can easily step down to the next level which is only about three feet or so. There's another level below that, about eight feet down but from there it's a steep drop. Like a lot of things in life, it's perfectly safe so long as you treat the Flow with respect." He looked at each of them in turn, as if trying to gauge whether they were thrilled or scared. "I tell you what, sit on the edge of the path and just look out. Hopefully you can forget your fears and drink in this glorious sight."

He went straight to the edge and sat down. Jo felt her stomach lurch. Martin sat next to him then glanced over his shoulder at her. "It's fine. The next level is just below us."

Jo stepped closer and, from this new angle, could see the next level of limestone extended out six or seven feet. She carefully sat next to Martin and he held her hand tightly.

"You're safe," he said.

She wasn't entirely comfortable but gave him what she hoped was a reassuring smile. "If you say so."

"You are. I won't let anything bad happen to you."

Chapter 13

Jo, Last Week

Carole didn't look at all happy when Jo met her in the swimming pool car park.

"I can't stop for a coffee tonight," she moaned.

"Is everything okay?" Jo asked with concern.

"Not really. My bloody ex was supposed to be taking his mother to Sainsbury's and has now cancelled on her so, of course, she asks me because there's nobody else to help and I can't say no, can I? Even though Wednesdays are my evening and I love having a coffee with you and Tim but…" She shook her head. "My bloody ex," she muttered.

Jo followed her into the building. "That's shitty," she said. "I'll make it up for you next week and buy us both cookies, how about that?"

"It's a lovely gesture," Carole said. "But I'm supposed to be losing weight and getting into shape."

"I'll make you swim an extra length."

The session went well and Jo pushed herself harder than she had the previous week. When she went into the foyer to bag a table at the coffee shop, she saw the place was packed again. One of the other swimmers from the group came towards her with a take-out coffee cup.

"Another bloody inter-schools thing," she muttered to Jo as she passed. "No room at the inn."

"Hey," said Tim. He laughed when she jumped slightly. "Sorry. I thought you'd heard me."

"Too many people chatting," she said and gestured towards the coffee shop.

"Shit, it's happening again?" He turned around. "And where's Carole?"

"She can't make it." Jo pulled a face. "We may have to call our coffee and chat off."

"Or we could go across the road," he said. "There's a place on the plaza behind the Newborough Centre called Ratty's. I've been there a couple of times with people from work."

"Sounds like a plan," she said.

"You're sure it's okay?"

"Why wouldn't it be?"

"Well, I just wanted to make sure. You know, just in case anyone saw us."

"In case anyone saw us going for a coffee?"

"No, I meant if any of your friends saw you going for a coffee with someone other than your husband."

"I am allowed other friends, you know," she said with a smile. "And what about you? Won't your wife mind?"

"I won't tell her," he said.

* * *

Jo liked Ratty's. The wood-panelled walls made her feel like she was in the middle of a posh drawing room from an Agatha Christie mystery while the leather chairs and sofas had a real lived-in look to them.

"You get a seat," Tim said, "and I'll order."

He gestured vaguely towards the far corner. Jo picked a small table with an oversized leather chair and a two-seater by the window. She sat on the two-seater.

Tim put the mugs on the table and sat on the chair across from her. "You look at home there."

"It's glorious."

"You've never been in here before?"

"Nope. Whenever I come shopping, either with Martin or my friends, we tend to use one of the coffee shops in the centre."

"You're missing out," Tim said. "So, I don't think you ever told me what Martin does for a living."

"He's a construction project manager."

"And how did you meet?"

"Through work. He was managing a site and my company supplied all the materials, so he and I were chatting on the phone fairly regularly and one thing led to another. How about you?"

"Linda was in the graphics department of a company where I set up a server and IT infrastructure. She was having some problems with her laptop and when I offered to help, we chatted and I discovered she had a wonderfully dry sense of humour. Which was something my ex-wife absolutely didn't have, so that was such a relief. Anyway, one day I went in and she'd designed me a business card that really made me laugh. On one side was a picture of a poorly looking computer and on the other it said TIM ITM."

He laughed and Jo felt slightly uncomfortable because she didn't get the joke. His laugh tapered away and he frowned. "Tim's obviously me and my job title is an anagram of Tim." He looked disappointed. "We thought it was funny."

"I might have got it quicker if I'd seen it."

"Of course."

"So, do you enjoy the job?"

"I do but, before you ask, it's not just a case of me telling people to turn their machine off and on again. If I had a penny for everyone who asked me that, I'd be driving a very nice middle-management grade German car."

She laughed at that.

"It can be good fun though. The best thing I ever saw was when me and my friend Phil were doing some bread-and-butter contract work installing drivers on desktop computers in a large office. Phil was a bit of a lad and we called him 'Yer Boots' because he had a foot fetish and loved nothing more than rooting around under all these desks. Most of the time the women would get out of the way, which he found disappointing…"

Jo already didn't like the sound of Phil. "I'd get out of the way if he was under my desk too."

"I suppose it could be creepy," he acknowledged, "but there was this one woman who stayed put and Phil was convinced she liked the idea of him under there, if you get what I mean. So he's doing his stuff and they've got the big bosses in who're getting a tour." He told her the anecdote and played up the humour so Jo found herself getting caught up in it. Tim got to his feet as he told her about the big boss so he could act out what he was describing. Jo laughed at the pantomime and that seemed to spur Tim on. Soon the story sounded more embellishment than truth but she was enjoying herself.

"And that's why Phil Yer Boots was never allowed back on the fifth floor!" Tim finished with a flourish then dropped onto the cushion next to her. "I love that story," he said.

"It's very good. How much of it is true?"

"It depends on how good the audience is," he said then looked at her. "Do you think Carole is lonely?"

Tim's abrupt change of pace took her by surprise. "I think she might be," she said diplomatically. "But a lot of people are, aren't they?"

"Maybe." He leaned across the table to get his drink then flopped back in the chair. "I am, sometimes. Aren't you?"

"Every now and again, especially since Olivia left."

"I feel like saying something to Carole but I don't want to sound like I'm preaching to her, you know?"

"What would you say to her?"

"That she's not alone." He sipped his drink. "The world's full of lonely people who are perhaps a bit scared to make the effort to connect."

"That might be true or it might be circumstance. Carole makes the effort to connect and has friends but she's juggling that with being a single mum."

"That's not how I see her."

There was a tone in his voice she couldn't quite place. Did he fancy Carole? Did he want her help in setting them up? "How do you see her, then?"

"As someone who wants to be part of something."

"Don't most of us want that?"

"Not my wife," he said in a flat voice.

He looked at her intently and Jo felt something nag at the back of her mind. She looked out of the window to break his gaze and saw a man leaning against a phone box. He was on his mobile but glanced at her then looked away without interest.

"How do you mean?" she asked.

"She doesn't understand me," Tim said.

'Oh no,' thought Jo. The nagging sensation got stronger. "I'm sure that's not the case." She leaned forward to get her own cup and took the opportunity to slide a little to one side to put some space between them.

"It is. She's so fixated on the baby thing that she's not really paying attention to me."

"Well, it's a big deal for her."

"It's a big deal for both of us," he corrected her. "I'm involved in all this, too."

"I didn't mean you weren't, but maybe she's feeling anxious because she can't fall pregnant."

"You see," he said and shifted so he faced her. "You understand me. I knew you did from the moment we met."

"I don't know about that." She tried to sound diplomatic. "Perhaps it's more that I can see the whole picture."

"No, it's because you get me." He edged towards her. "It's so rare to find someone so on your wavelength."

The nagging became a full-on cry. "I don't think we want to be having this conversation, Tim."

"I do," he said and touched the back of her hand. She pulled it away and he looked hurt. "Would you rather do this somewhere else?"

"No," she said with horror. "I'd rather not do this at all." How had she got herself into this position?

"I'm only saying what we're both feeling," he said with a slight smile.

"Honestly, Tim, you're not." She stood up quickly but had to move towards the window to get around the table.

"Don't go," he said and stood up, effectively boxing her in. "You're misunderstanding me."

"I hope so." She tried to push down the sensation of feeling trapped and looked around. Half a dozen of the tables were occupied and there were two baristas behind the counter. "I need to get going. I'll see you next week."

"No, you won't, Jo, and we both know it. You're going to be weird with me now and ruin everything."

"I won't." She didn't want to cause a scene, but she would happily do so if this got out of hand. "Thank you for the coffee."

"I know we've got a connection," he muttered.

She couldn't think of a good way to answer that. She grabbed her bag and pushed past him, then made her way out of Ratty's. As she closed the door behind her she saw Tim flop back into the chair.

Jo pulled her coat on against the chilly evening air as she crossed the plaza and angled towards the swimming pool. The lights had come on around the building and across the car park.

"Bastard," she muttered as she picked up her pace. She felt foolish for putting herself into the situation but she was angry, too, that he'd invaded her space and made her feel bad. How dare he? He knew she was married and if he felt ignored and unloved at home, he had no right to project anything onto her.

She waited at the kerb for a couple of cars to go by and glanced over her shoulder to make sure he hadn't decided to follow her and press his case. She couldn't see him. The man she'd seen by the telephone box was walking across the plaza in her direction.

Once the road was clear, she crossed and took several deep breaths to calm herself down.

The only thing he'd been right about this evening was that she was going to be weird with him from now on. She'd ring Carole later and say there was no way she'd be joining Tim for coffee ever again.

Jo followed the path past the pool entrance and around the side of the building towards the almost full car park. Most of the vehicles were empty but a few were occupied by people whose faces were lit by phone screens. Nobody looked up as she walked by. A car was parked at the corner with the window down. The driver sat with his arm out, a cigarette between his fingers as he listened to heavy metal music. She passed his car and went to the left towards the well-lit corner where she and Carole had got into the habit of parking.

Her nerves jangled when she heard footsteps. She glanced over her shoulder and saw Tim about fifty yards behind her. The shock of it seemed to beat in all her pulse points.

"Don't worry yourself," he said. "We're both parked here."

She could barely bring herself to speak to him. "Where's your car?"

"Wouldn't you like to know?" he asked with a sneer.

Jo didn't respond because that would just re-open their dialogue and the last thing he needed now was an olive branch. She walked briskly to her car and tried to focus on it rather than listen to his footsteps get closer.

"Do you think you're too good for me or something?" He sounded very close.

"What're you doing, Tim?" She stopped and reached into her coat pocket for her car keys. Her heart thudded as she palmed them and put the barrel between her fingers.

"I asked if you thought you were too good for me?"

She turned to face him. "No, Tim, but we're both married."

"You should be flattered I'm interested. You're ten years older than me."

The barb was unpleasant but didn't sting. "I'm not flattered, trust me. You made a mistake and you're now making it worse, so let's leave it at that."

"I haven't made a mistake. I've seen the way you look at me."

She bit the inside of her cheek but didn't want him to see or hear any fear in her. "I look at you the same way I look at Carole and I don't fancy her either."

He shook his head. "You're not very nice, are you?"

There were more footsteps and she looked over Tim's shoulder as the cigarette-smoking man walked over. He wasn't very tall and his T-shirt struggled to contain his belly. "Everything alright here?" He didn't pay any attention to Tim at all.

"Yes thanks," Jo said. "Tim was just going to his car."

Tim glanced at the man then back at Jo. "You're a cold bitch, aren't you?"

She pursed her lips. "You're making a lot of mistakes this evening, you sad man."

"So you say. But one day you'll be on your own and when you turn around, I'll be there. I'll sort you out."

"Don't threaten me, you twat. Why don't you just fuck off?"

Her retort seemed to surprise him and he turned on his heel to stalk away. Jo and the other man watched him until he got into his car and started the engine. She felt hot and nauseous.

"Are you okay?" the man asked. "I thought you probably had it under control but I've got a mother and two daughters and when I see a bloke squaring up to a woman I can't look away."

"I'm fine. But thank you."

"No worries, love. And I hope your hand's in your pocket because you're gripping your car keys."

"I am."

He laughed. "Good on you. Take it easy, love."

"I will, thank you."

Jo quickly got into the car and locked the doors. Her adrenaline wore off and left her like a wet rag. She leaned against the head rest until the feeling passed and her breathing steadied. She'd handled him as well as she could and, even though her Good Samaritan helped, she thought she'd bettered Tim. It was still fucking scary, though.

And his words were burrowing into her head.

'When you turn around, I'll be there.'

The thought of it made her shiver.

Chapter 14

Peter allowed them ten minutes to drink in the beauty of the valley before calling them over to set up camp.

"The limestone base drops here," he said and stepped onto patchy grass. He walked around a small bowl shape in the ground, lined with rocks. Jo saw ashes and small, half-burned sticks in the base of it. Two holes were set diametrically across from one another on either side of the bowl.

"This is the firepit," Peter said. "Once the sun goes down it'll get chilly, so the fire gives us some illumination, a lot of heat and a means to cook dinner."

"Sounds good to me," said Tony. "I'm starving."

"Then you'll enjoy the hearty stew I made for us this morning."

"Brilliant," said Martin. "I feel like I've walked a marathon."

"Most of it was uphill," said Sam. "I'm ready for a break."

A row of large rocks had been set into a semi-circle on the other side of the firepit. Peter put his rucksack down by one of them "This is where we sit and talk and eat," he said. "Unfortunately, we have a bit of work to do before then. We need to make camp and collect firewood and get dinner on the go before we lose the sun."

"I don't mind putting tents up," said Martin.

"Nor me," said Tony. "Where are they?"

"In a brick store in those woods," Peter said and pointed towards trees that bordered the back end of the plateau. "The food's there too."

"I'm happy to collect firewood," said Jo, who didn't relish the idea of cooking for six in these conditions.

"I'll go with you," Sam chipped in.

"Excellent," said Peter. "That leaves me and Gayle to prepare the food and get started."

"What about toilet facilities?" Martin asked.

"You'll be happy to hear you won't have to dig out latrines for yourselves." Peter smiled at everyone's positive reaction. "We already have some set up in the woods. They're not luxurious in the slightest and we work on the principle our hikers clean as they go so if you make a mess then don't expect someone else to deal with it." He looked at Jo with a big smile. "Dinner will be an hour after we've got the fire blazing."

"No pressure, then," said Jo.

"Not if you go now," Martin said.

* * *

The woods were dark enough that Jo and Sam had to use their torch apps as they walked along the narrow trail.

"Should we leave a trail of breadcrumbs to make sure we find our way out?" he asked.

She laughed. "I think we'll be fine."

"How much wood should we gather?"

"No idea. It's not a question I get asked very often."

"Curious, that."

"How's the filming going?"

"Not too bad. I just wish I could get it all uploaded safely."

"Is this for your YouTube channel?"

"Kind of. I like to think of myself as a content creator. It's something I've wanted to do for my whole life."

"How old are you?"

"Twenty-six," he said. "When I was younger, I used my dad's camera and made a lot of Pokémon clips and stuff with FIFA. Now I'm looking at doing some documentaries."

"What kind of documentaries?"

"Stuff I find interesting. My channel has a relatively stable subscriber base but I need to try and build it. So I'm making a film about Gayle and her goals, because she's fascinating and beautiful and probably my best friend. Plus, she's smarter and sexier than she thinks she is."

Jo wondered if Gayle had ever heard him talk about her like this.

"I thought putting Gayle in front of this great scenery would work really well with her Insta profile, so it's a win-win."

"You like her a lot, don't you?"

He didn't answer immediately and she thought he seemed embarrassed. "Honestly? I fancy her something rotten, Jo, but to be honest, I'm not sure she knows I exist in that way."

"Well," she said carefully, "sometimes friendships are a wonderful thing."

"Yeah," he said. "That's what my dad reckons, too." He bent over to pick up a short log. "Is this big enough, do you think?"

"Probably," she said. "I don't really know but if they're waiting for us to start cooking we need to get some more."

They collected for another five minutes and when she was holding half a dozen logs or so, Jo stopped and blew her fringe out of her eyes. "Let's head back."

Sam had gathered more logs than her and seemed to be having trouble holding them. "While they're cooking, I'll see if I can find a signal."

"Have you still not found one?"

"No. I'm starting to wonder whether Peter was having us on when he said it was patchy. You read all these things about military jamming devices being developed, it makes me wonder if this whole moor is a blackspot."

"Could you not wait until we get back to the hotel?"

"I could but I wouldn't want to lose any footage if something happened to the camera. It'd be good to know we can contact people, too. I mean, what would have happened if Gayle had been hurt earlier?"

"Peter has a satellite phone."

"And he was racing around on the scree at the time." He shook his head. "You were fantastic there, too. I feel so guilty that I didn't do anything."

"Sometimes people freeze."

"It didn't help that I thought it was funny at first and Gayle saw me laughing as she slid away. But I thought we could send the clip to FailArmy and make a bit out of it."

A sudden thought hit Jo. "You filmed it all?"

"Most of it, why?"

"Will you show me the footage when we get back?"

"Of course."

* * *

Martin and Tony had the first tent half up by the time they got back to the plateau and Gayle and Peter were sitting on the rocks sorting through a couple of cardboard boxes. Peter directed Jo and Sam to put the logs into the firepit.

"Nice work," he said. "You found a good load."

"Not bad for city slickers, eh?" Jo asked.

"Well," he said and tipped her a wink. "There could have been more."

She laughed and protested and he smiled broadly as he took three cubes of firelighter and a small metal tin with 'petrol' written on it from one of the boxes.

"Did you get all this stuff out the store?" Jo asked.

"Yes. I know it's a bit of a cheat but it saves us having to lug everything with us. You remember I told you about the farm with the lovely eggs? Well, the supplies get delivered there and the farmer's son puts it in the store for me."

"And better than all that…" hinted Gayle. She reached into the other box and pulled out two bottles of wine.

"You really do think of everything," Jo said. "I'm impressed."

"I try," said Peter. He laid the firelighter blocks on the wood and squirted some of the petrol on too. The fire was blazing within moments. He fashioned three metal rods into a tripod and set them up over the firepit then hung a metal bowl from the centre.

Sam tapped Jo's hand. "Did you want to have a look at that footage?"

"Yes."

She got her glasses from her rucksack then followed him to sit on the edge of the Flow.

"There'll be sound," he said, "but it'll be tinny."

"Not to worry, I just want to see something."

"Like whether or not Tony really tripped?"

She shot him a surprised look. "Did you see it?"

"No, but I had a similar thought." He manipulated the GoPro then held it so they could both see the screen. He pressed play.

The image was crisp as it panned steadily from the side of Black Shuck Hill to look across the slab towards Jo and

Gayle. Tony was between Sam and the two women and picked his way slowly from one gap to the next. He glanced over his shoulder in Sam's direction and seemed surprised to see him filming, then looked towards Jo. He shifted forward quickly as if he'd started running and although she could see him raise his arms he effectively blocked her from view. She watched the collision and winced as she recalled the force of the impact.

Sam rewound the film and played it again. "He doesn't trip, does he?"

"No. But is he stumbling or running?"

They played the few seconds over a few times but she couldn't decide. In her mind, she wanted to say he was running into her but that wasn't exactly what the video showed.

"What does he look at before he moves?" she asked.

"I don't know. It looks like it's at me, but it wasn't. Maybe he heard something and lost his balance when he glanced over."

"It's not clear, is it?" she asked reluctantly.

"No, but it's an odd way to fall."

"Yeah, that's what I thought. And did you see anything of the bald man he said he saw up the hill?"

"Nope, not a sign."

"Strange that," she said. "I wonder where he went?"

Chapter 15

The sun was setting by the time they finished eating Peter's delicious stew and clouds were gathering in the darkening sky.

"A dinner on a cliff with new friends is always a good thing," said Peter and raised his tin cup of wine to the party.

Jo raised her own as Martin said, "Hear, hear," and the others joined in the salute.

Tony put his plate on the ground between his feet and looked up at the sky. "Do you think we're going to get rain?"

"So the Met Office says," Peter said. He checked his watch. "They reckon it'll start around ten o'clock and last for a couple of hours so if we're in our tents by then, we should be fine."

Martin got up and stretched. "I feel like I've eaten too much," he said.

"Me too," said Tony. He walked to the firepit and put his hands out to warm them against the flames.

"You can't be cold," said Sam.

"I'm not," he said and sat next to Gayle on the boulder. It looked to Jo like the young woman almost curled up on herself. Sam, sitting on the other side of Gayle, didn't seem to notice.

Tony turned to the young woman next to him. "I hope you don't get cold through the night either, Gayle."

"I'm sure I won't," she said.

"I hope young Sammy can keep you warm."

Jo was surprised at his brazenness and glanced at Martin. He watched the exchange closely.

"So, what's the plan for tomorrow?" Jo asked. She'd taken her boots off and was flexing her toes in front of the fire.

Peter stretched his legs out. His boots still looked far too big for his legs. "Well, the first option is a straight hike back to Hadley Hall of about eight miles. It's a slow uphill gradient so you'll know you've walked it, but it isn't too taxing and the scenery will more than compensate. The second is the same but we stop off at my friend's farm for some of her free-range-egg sandwiches."

"I vote for the second," said Martin.

"I like a man who thinks with his belly," said Peter. "We can decide in the morning."

He gathered the plates and put them into one of the cardboard boxes then carried it back towards the wood.

Tony went to his tent and Sam began to walk around the plateau with his phone held aloft. Gayle leaned back on her rock and looked towards the sky. Jo and Martin walked towards the cliff edge. She leaned her head against his shoulder and the closeness felt good.

"I'm enjoying this," she said.

"So am I, other than your little incident this afternoon."

"I'd hardly call it little," she said and told him about Sam's clip.

"I did say at the time it was an accident."

"I know."

If Martin heard the doubt in her voice he didn't acknowledge it. "Well, all that lies between us and a weekend of pampered luxury is a night under canvas and an eight-mile hike tomorrow."

"I can do that," she said.

They sat together on the edge. The sky was almost purple with shades of pink streaking through it. It felt to Jo like it had been a long time since she last saw a sunset so vivid.

"It's a glorious sight," he said. "And so are you."

She laughed at his corny line and he joined in with her.

"This is going to work, Jo." He squeezed her hand. "I know things haven't been right for a while but that'll change after this. You watch."

She put her free hand over his. "I believe you, Martin."

He kissed her and she thought for a moment it was going to become more but he leaned back to look at her intently. "We don't have to wait until the hotel to start pampering one another," he said softly.

"You wouldn't rather wait for a nice bed in a glamorous hotel room?"

He gave her a saucy grin. "How about in a chilly tent on a thin ground sheet?"

"Hmmm," she said, as if pretending to consider his offer. "Maybe I'll pass on that."

"Spoilsport," he said with a pout. "Come on, the light's fading. Let's get back to camp."

Chapter 16

Martin, Seven Weeks Ago

"Martin! You need to come to shed seven, quick. We're in trouble."

His installation manager, Gordy, sounded panicked and that was unusual enough to be troubling. "What's the matter? Is anyone hurt?"

"Not yet."

What did 'not yet' mean? Gordy normally called a spade a spade, so his elusiveness was worrying. "I'll be there as quick as I can."

It was after eight on a Friday night so most of the workers had left hours ago to start spending their pay. The only people on site were with a small crew in the main warehouse working on control panels and Gordy wasn't with them. Martin rushed out to his car and drove as quickly as he could along the service road and around the back of the massive warehouse to the Norris Construction compound.

It was surrounded by a chain-link fence and overhead lights stood at each corner with six containers for storage and a small mobile unit that served as the installation manager's office. Three cars were parked alongside it, which was strictly against site policy. One of them was a black Range Rover and Martin didn't need to see the private number plate to know it belonged to Murray Norris.

Why would Norris be here? He rarely came to site and always made a point of dropping in to see Martin whenever he did. These days he preferred to keep his hands clean as he moved in executive circles and groomed his son, Will, to take over the family business. Norris was a self-made millionaire who didn't suffer fools gladly but Will was a real prick. Entitled and dim, he spent more time creating problems than doing anything constructive, but Norris wouldn't hear a word against him. Martin parked alongside the Range Rover and got out. He zipped up his parka against the chill in the air.

Martin pulled open the door and went into the office that was designed for use rather than comfort. Will Norris stood against the back wall with his arms folded. He jutted his chin towards Martin. Had Will borrowed his dad's car?

Four of the desks had been moved to form a large table and half a dozen men sat at it, Gordy amongst them. The table was laden with beer cans and piles of gambling chips. Martin groaned.

"A card school?" he asked, looking from Gordy to Will.

"Yeah," said Will with a grin that made you want to wipe it off roughly. "Allowing gambling and drinking on your site isn't a good look, Martin."

"I didn't know anything about this, Will." Martin glared at Gordy who couldn't manage anything more than a feeble shrug.

"That doesn't sound good either." Will looked like he was enjoying himself.

None of the gamblers would meet Martin's gaze except Gordy. "What the fuck, Gordy?" he asked.

A cistern flushed and Martin looked towards the toilet door. It opened as Jerry, one of Norris' minders, came through. His dark chinos struggled to contain his thighs and his shirt was tight over his biceps. Martin waited. If Jerry was here then so was Norris and that meant this evening was going to get worse.

Norris came into the office a moment later. He wore a dark suit with the shirt unbuttoned at the neck and no tie. His steel-grey hair was smoothly combed back. He was wiping his hands on a paper towel and it was his fingers that gave away the fact he'd worked his way up to this position. They were rough and calloused beyond the restorative powers of any manicure. He feigned surprise at seeing Martin.

"Mr Harper," he said with a smile like a shark about to feast.

"Mr Norris."

"So nice to see you."

"I didn't realise you were on site, Murray."

"So it seems." He gestured towards the card game. "You do know this is against site and company policy, don't you?"

"I do," Martin said. There was no point protesting his innocence.

"If the HSE got wind of this then we'd all be for the high jump. And for it to happen under your nose without your knowledge reflects really badly on you."

"I know," said Martin. He and Norris went back a long way but this was business and if Martin had to be thrown to the wolves to save the company then Murray Norris wouldn't hesitate for a second.

Norris looked around until he found a waste bin and dropped the paper towel into it. "Good." He walked towards the card table. "So, what're we going to do about this?"

Jerry took a slow walk around the room watching the gamblers.

"It's a serious breach," said Martin. "We'll fire the organisers and the rest will be given final written warnings."

"So who is the organiser?" Norris asked.

"I don't know that yet, Murray."

"We need to get to the bottom of this, don't we?" Norris nodded towards his son and Will moved so he stood behind Gordy.

"How about you?" Will asked as he slapped his hands hard on Gordy's shoulders.

Gordy kept looking at Martin. "Not me," he said.

"But you're the installations manager and this is your office," Will pointed out.

Gordy twisted in his seat. "And you're one of the project managers, Will, and you've been coming to these sessions for the past couple of months."

"For fuck's sake," muttered Norris.

"Hold on," said Martin to Will. "Are you saying you knew these sessions were taking place and didn't tell me?"

Will shrugged. "Must have slipped my mind."

"It probably slipped because of the losing streak you've been on since you started," said Gordy.

Martin looked at Norris. "So you're here because Will told you about it?"

"These bastards have fleeced him out of about thirty grand, so yes, I'm here because he told me."

"He's old enough to deal with this on his own if he wants to."

Norris bared his teeth for the briefest of moments and struggled to keep his voice under control. "I think your suggestion is correct but if any of those fuckers, any single one, goes to the HSE and gets this project shut down, there'll be massive trouble." The anger seemed to come off him in waves. "Sort it out, Harper."

Martin walked over to the table. The men seated behind it looked at him with a mixture of worry and concern. "What's going on, Gordy?"

"You know he's going to sack all of us, don't you?" Gordy asked. "After we've paid back Junior's money. And I haven't got the money."

"Did you organise it?"

"No, and I'm not going to tell you who did. I won't give Willy Wonka back here the pleasure."

"You miserable fucker," said Will and pulled Gordy to his feet.

Gordy went with the momentum and punched Will's shoulder hard. Will made an odd sound and then Jerry grabbed Gordy by the throat and pushed him into the wall hard enough that the entire office shook.

"Hey," said Martin and moved around the table.

Jerry lifted Gordy until his feet were in the air. He made horrible gurgling noises and clawed uselessly at Jerry's big hand.

"He said it wasn't him." Martin pulled on Jerry's arm. "Let him go."

"Do it," said Norris.

Jerry did as he was told. Gordy landed in a heap and sucked in air.

"I haven't got time for this," said Norris and jabbed a finger at Martin. "Get this fucker sacked and the others away. Jerry, you know what to do."

Jerry pulled Gordy to his feet and dragged him across the room.

"Don't take him anywhere," Martin demanded. "Murray, don't do this. We can sort it out."

"Oh, can we? I'd ask if you have the thirty grand he owes my boy but of course you don't because your girl's at university and that's costing you. I need to teach Gordy a lesson and send everyone else the message that they can't mess me around. Nothing signals that better than broken bones."

"It's a fucking card school, Murray. This isn't a war with another company."

"If that's what my dad wants then we'll break as many bones as we need to," Will said excitedly. He looked like he was enjoying this far more than was healthy. "I'll come and watch."

Gordy struggled to free himself from Jerry's grip as he was dragged across the office towards the door. "Help me, Martin," he said.

Martin confronted Norris. "This is madness."

"You're right," said Norris. "If he can't work, he can't pay, so only break a hand and a leg."

Will giggled.

"This isn't going to happen, Murray," said Martin.

"Yes, it is, Harper. It's my site you're bringing into disrepute and I won't stand for it, do you hear me? You're a good site man but right now you're a pain the arse. You're fired. Will can replace you."

"Are you serious? A trained chimp would be better."

Norris leaned in close. "Are you calling my boy an idiot?"

"Yes, I am."

Norris tried to push Martin away. "Get the fuck off my site, Harper."

"Or what?" Martin asked.

"Have him, Dad," said Will.

"Shut up," Norris shouted. "This is all your fucking fault and I've got to clear up the mess."

"Let Gordy go and I'll sort this out," Martin said. "We're all reasonable men here."

"You're a fool, Harper, and you always were. Jerry, take him out and break some bones."

"No," said Martin.

Norris grabbed for him and there was a confusion of arms and hands. Norris dug his fingers into Martin's throat and Martin threw a punch as best he could. It connected hard with Norris' jaw and the man staggered back and collapsed onto a drawing table.

Will shrieked and Jerry let go of Gordy and went to help his boss. Norris shook his head to clear it as he slowly got to his feet. "You're finished," he said.

"Have him, Dad," implored Will.

"No," said Norris and rubbed his jaw. "There are more ways to skin a cat. Get the fuck off my site, Harper, and take your mates with you. If I see any of you near this place or Will in the future, you'll all have your legs broken."

Martin was running on adrenaline and tension pulled his muscles tight. "Get out of here," he told the gamblers and they almost fell over one another in their haste to leave. He grabbed Gordy's arm and pulled him through the door.

Outside it felt colder than ever and Martin steadied himself on the banister for a moment.

"What now, Martin?" Gordy asked.

"We walk away," he said. "You've just cost me a lot of money, you fucking idiot."

"I'm sorry."

"Yeah, I'll bet you are."

Gordy looked broken. "But thanks for standing up for me like that. Not many blokes would have."

"Even if you're an idiot, I can't stand by while you get bones broken."

Martin got into his car and watched Gordy drive away. It felt like a weight was compressing his lungs. How was he going to explain this to Jo?

Chapter 17

Tony was drinking from a can and offered the remains of a four-pack to Martin as he and Jo walked back to the firepit.

"I brought two of these with me," he said. "Did either of you good people want one?"

"No thanks," said Jo.

"Sure," said Martin. "I never thought to bring booze."

Tony tossed a can to Martin as Sam ambled over. He was carrying his own can and turned to watch Gayle come over from the trees.

"Hey," he said with a slight slur.

"Oh, are you getting drunk?" she asked.

"I don't think so," Sam said and frowned at Tony. "I've only had one can."

"He has indeed." Tony flashed Gayle a smile as if to point out what a lightweight Sam was.

Martin held up his can to read it. "It's a strong beer though, mate, so take your time."

"Is it?" Tony asked innocently. He checked his own can. "So it is."

"Maybe you should take it easy," Gayle said to Sam.

"Maybe you should let the lad decide for himself," Tony suggested.

* * *

Tony had a pack of cards and, as the evening wore on, they played a selection of games. Martin, Tony and Sam worked their way through the beer while Jo and Gayle stuck with the wine. Peter had one more and then sipped from his water bottle after that.

The wine gave Jo enough of a pleasant buzz that she felt good without the threat of a heavy head tomorrow. "It was a good idea to bring the wine."

"Another stroke of genius from my good lady wife," Peter said.

"You should have put beer in there, too," said Tony. "Lanky Lad here will drink us out of house and home." He handed another can to Sam who took it with a dreamy look.

"Please don't drink any more," Gayle said.

"You keep getting onto me," Sam slurred and sounded wounded. "I'm fine."

"He says he's fine," said Martin. He'd drunk two of the cans but they didn't seem to have affected him.

Jo gave him a look.

"What?" he asked, confused.

"Don't," she said.

"Why not? It's funny. The lad wants to have a drink."

"It's up to me," said Sam.

"Too right, mate," said Tony. "You tell them. Don't let yourself get under the thumb now or you'll never get out."

"He's not under the thumb," muttered Gayle. "But he's not a big drinker."

Jo felt for Gayle and was getting more annoyed with Tony, and also Martin, for enabling him. She didn't know what Tony was playing at but he seemed intent on stirring the pot and she didn't like it. She didn't like him much, either. She looked at Peter for back-up and he gave her a curt nod.

"Maybe you need to take it a little bit easy, Sam," Peter said. "We've got a good hike tomorrow and you don't want to be feeling under the weather."

Sam looked from Peter to the can and back. "You could be right," he said.

"He is right," urged Gayle.

"Nah, you do what you want, mate," said Tony.

"Why don't you just leave him alone?" Gayle asked. "You've been on at him all day."

"It's only a bit of a laugh," Tony protested without conviction.

"Except none of the rest of us are laughing," Jo said.

His smile was tight-lipped and felt horribly cold but she held his gaze. He looked away a few moments later to her relief.

"I'm okay," said Sam and got unsteadily to his feet. "See? No problem." He rocked back and sat heavily. "Whoops."

Gayle shook her head.

Peter made a show of looking at his watch. "How about we play one more hand of cards then call it a night?"

Tony leaned forward and handed him the deck. "You know what, Peter? As much as I appreciate it, I think I'm going to sit this one out. I don't like playing with spoilsports."

Martin got up. "No, don't go off."

The tension in the air was getting heavier all the time but Jo didn't want to let Tony off, especially since all this was his fault. "Leave him," she said.

"Nah, don't go, mate," said Sam. "Let's have another round."

"Let him go," Gayle said to Sam. "He wants to."

Tony got up and held out his hands. "Look, I'm sorry if I've caused any hassle. I didn't mean to and, let's face it, it's not my fault Lanky Lad can't hold his booze, is it?"

Gayle looked like she was about to say something but Peter put a hand on her arm and she bit her lip.

"Why do you keep pushing?" Jo asked.

Tony smiled slyly. "I'm sorry, okay. I keep apologising but it's never enough for you. I was just messing about because I thought we all fancied a laugh."

"It's okay, mate," said Martin. "Everything'll be better in the morning."

"I doubt it," Tony said and he walked into the darkness towards the tents.

"Thank fuck for that," said Gayle.

"Hey, hang on a minute," said Martin. "Whether it was the right thing or not, Sam chose to have that booze. Tony hardly forced him, did he?"

"Come on, Martin," said Jo. "He's clearly had enough."

"He's not a big drinker," said Gayle.

"And is that Tony's fault too?"

"No," said Peter. His voice was calm and level, a perfect peacekeeper. "Why don't we call it quits for tonight and get Sam to drink some water? I have some paracetamol in my rucksack if his head is splitting in the morning."

"Are we going to sleep now?" Sam asked. He got to his feet and made a retching sound.

"Oh no," said Gayle. "You useless bloody lump."

"I'm completely fine."

"No, you're not. This is embarrassing."

"It's really not, Gayle," said Peter. "You're both young. I'm sure Martin and I have similar tales from when we were in our twenties." He looked hopefully at Martin. "Don't we?"

Martin smiled. "A fair few."

"And I wouldn't want to suggest anything untoward of Jo but…"

"Yes," Jo said. "A few."

"You see?" Peter said. "It's fine."

"I'm sorry," said Sam and retched again.

"I'm not having this," said Gayle. "Drunk people are the worst when you're almost sober and if you're sick everywhere then you're going to make me throw up. You can sleep out here."

"That's not very nice," Sam said. "Why are you being horrible?"

"I'm not," she said.

"He can't sleep out there," said Peter. "He'll get hypothermia."

"Peter's right," said Jo. She sympathised with Gayle but they couldn't leave Sam out in the elements.

"I know he is." Gayle's eyes glistened in the light of the fire. "But it's not fair."

"No," said Jo. She moved around to sit next to Gayle and held her hand. "We'll figure something out."

"Can I sleep in with you?" Gayle asked.

"Well, I'm not sure…"

"What about me?" Sam asked. "We're supposed to be sleeping together tonight."

"Not with you in that state," she muttered then looked at Jo. "I'm sorry, it was a stupid question. Just ignore me."

"It's not that…" Jo looked at Martin who raised his eyebrows in a query. "Would you mind if Gayle shared our tent with me and you had Sam in with you?"

"Why would I want to do that? I didn't get him drunk. If he's going to share with anyone, why can't it be Tony? Or Peter?"

"I have a one-man tent, or he'd be welcome," said Peter softly.

"Of course you do," said Martin. "Well, I'll go and wake Tony up then."

"He's probably heard everything anyway," said Jo.

"Yeah," Martin said. He looked towards the tents then shook his head. "Fuck it," he muttered. "Okay, I'll go in with him." He didn't look at all happy about the decision. "If he pukes though, he's out."

"Thank you," Jo said. "I'll make it up to you once we get to Hadley Hall."

"Yeah, yeah. You realise I'm going to hold you to that, don't you?"

"I would hope so," she said and pulled him into a hug that he seemed reluctant to reciprocate at first but then he kissed her.

"You're too nice for your own good," he said.

"I know."

He retrieved his sleeping bag from their tent then came back for Sam and helped him to his feet. "Come on, mate," he said.

Chapter 18

The tent wasn't very big but they'd set up their sleeping bags so they top-and-tailed with the rucksacks between them and their coats on top. Jo's feet were by the opening and as she crawled into her bag after zipping the tent closed the rain began.

She clicked off her torch app once she was settled and the darkness was absolute. It took a while for her vision to adjust and even then, she could only make out various shapes in the gloom.

"Wow," said Gayle. "I didn't think it was going to be quite this dark, did you?"

"No, but the fact it's cloudy and raining doesn't help."

After a few moments the rain hit the canvas like hailstones and she was glad the tent and ground sheet were both waterproof.

"Thank you again for doing this, Jo. I really do appreciate you giving up your night with Martin."

"Don't worry. I know what it's like trying to get to sleep next to someone who's drunk. How are you feeling now?"

"Better," Gayle said. "I've been doing some mindfulness exercises and trying to focus on the night sounds and that's calming me down."

"I'm glad to hear it." She hadn't said anything, but Jo did wonder what the mood of the group would be like tomorrow, bearing in mind how quickly the evening had soured.

"I'll bet the others think I'm silly for overreacting like that, but I have problems with drunks." She was quiet for a moment. "My mother started drinking heavily when my dad left us. She took to it with a vengeance and it wasn't ideal for fifteen-year-old me to be putting her to bed three or four nights a week, then getting up early the next morning to make sure she was ready for work before I went to school. And Sam knew this. He's only met her once or twice, but he knows what she's like and how I feel about it."

"He did have Tony and Martin egging him on, though."

"True. Tony was the worst. There's just something about that man, like he's pretending to be someone other than who he is. I mean, he puts me on edge with his smutty comments and those sly smiles, like we've got a secret and he's dying to tell everyone else."

Although her opinion of the man wasn't quite so dark, Jo didn't disagree and wished she'd been more forthright in shutting Tony up. "It's not just you," she said. "Stick with me tomorrow morning and we'll block him out."

"That's not fair on you and Martin, though." Gayle sighed. "Like this isn't."

"We've got the weekend for us. I'd rather make sure you're safe."

"You're lovely," Gayle said. "You really are. Olivia is a lucky girl to have a mum like you."

"I know. I keep telling her that but I don't think she believes me."

Gayle laughed. "You're funny, too."

"She hasn't said that for a while, I have to say."

They lapsed into a comfortable silence and Jo turned onto her side and closed her eyes. She could feel the miles of the day settling into her muscles and looked forward to a long, hot soothing bath when they got to the hotel.

"Goodnight, Jo. And thanks for everything, especially your advice. I didn't say anything to Sam about us not being together but I will. I have to think of myself, don't I?"

"You do, Gayle. As for the advice, you're welcome. I'll see you in the morning."

She expected to fall asleep quickly but heard Gayle's breathing slow into a steady rhythm before she succumbed.

* * *

Jo awoke with a start and, in her half-asleep state, panicked for a moment because everything seemed wrong until she remembered she was in a tent. The rain had eased off and Gayle was snoring lightly.

She rolled onto her side and touched the face of her Garmin watch and the display, big enough to read without her glasses, informed her it was a little before three. She closed her eyes then something brushed against the side of the tent, startling her. Footsteps moved away as if someone was making their way to the latrines.

Rather them than me, she thought, hoping against hope her bladder held up until there was at least some daylight.

She was on the verge of nodding off again when Gayle made a snuffling sound and said, "What was that light?"

"I was just checking my watch. Sorry, I didn't mean to wake you."

"It wasn't you, I don't think. I heard something. What time is it?"

Jo told her then heard Gayle sit up. "Are you okay?"

"I need to pee. I think that wine went straight through me." Gayle got out of her sleeping bag and Jo watched her silhouette pick up a jacket and put it on as best she could in the cramped conditions. "I'll see you in a bit."

"Be careful."

"I will. And I promise to be quiet when I come back so I don't wake you up."

Having endured Olivia's almost constant round of parties during the summer months, Jo was well used to being woken up however quiet the latecomer thought she was being. "Don't worry. Just make sure you walk straight out of the tent and go forwards. Keep away from the cliff."

"Yes, mum," Gayle said and unzipped the flap and went out. "See you later."

"Take care," Jo said and closed her eyes again.

Chapter 19

Martin, Six Weeks Ago

In the aftermath of Friday night, Martin made three mistakes which seemed very small at the time but grew until they threatened almost everything in his life.

The first was down to the fact he wasn't great with money. In his twenties he'd been persuaded to buy into a company that almost immediately went bankrupt and that killed his credit score. He'd also enjoyed a flutter on the horses. As the lone parent of an eight-year-old, a run of bad luck meant he'd had to borrow money there was no way to repay. When he met Jo, he was almost five thousand pounds in the hole and he'd tried to hide it from her. Thankfully for him, she was smart and quickly found out. They talked it through and she offered to help him financially on the strict understanding he didn't gamble again. He promised her he wouldn't and when they moved in together it was decided that she would look after the money. He'd managed to stick to his promise for the most part but still couldn't resist the odd flutter here and there. It was, he found, just a case of being careful not to gamble too much.

So even though the card school wasn't his fault, he worried that Jo might think he'd slipped into his old ways and then discover he hadn't kept his promise in the first place. He barely slept that first night and the next morning she was up early to do a host of Saturday errands, then Olivia rang with an issue it appeared only Jo could help her with. Martin paced like a cage animal, wary his window of opportunity was narrowing all the time. If he told her quickly, he might be able to convince her things had got out of his control, but even that wasn't certain.

How did he explain something that should have been so easily fixable? Murray Norris took delight in making things more complicated than they should be, especially when he was extracting a pound of flesh in a deal. Perhaps that was part of it. The fact he'd so quickly suggested Will taking over the job made Martin think all this had been preplanned, with Norris senior biding his time for the perfect moment, which Gordy's card school had handed to him on a plate. Martin's punch was the icing on the cake. Even if everything else could be ironed out or somehow ignored, he'd assaulted his boss and Norris would never forget that.

The other option was to say nothing. Why worry Jo if he didn't have to? If he lined himself up something else, then he could tell her he'd had enough of working for Norris and decided to move on.

Martin's second mistake was not properly grasping what Norris meant when he'd said 'there are more ways to skin a cat.' After the fact, Martin should have known something was wrong when he couldn't get a reply from any of the old contacts he rang over the weekend.

It wasn't until Monday when he left home at the usual time but went to Asda and found himself a table in the coffee shop that he fully understood.

He rang Connor Elliot, who he'd known since they worked on a car plant installation near Birmingham a few years ago. They'd had a good relationship and Connor told him to keep in touch. "It's Martin Harper."

"Ah."

It wasn't the response Martin had expected. "Is everything okay?"

"That all depends on why you're ringing," said Connor cagily.

"Just a catch-up really and to see if you had any projects coming up."

"I understood you were at Norris Construction."

"Yeah, I was project managing a big warehouse job in Hadlington."

"That's what I thought." Connor cleared his throat. "Listen, Martin, it's nothing personal but we've got a problem. Or, at least, you have."

"What's that?"

"You've been blackballed."

The word hit him like a punch. "You're kidding me?"

"Not about something like this, mate. What the fuck did you do?"

"I didn't…" He stopped. Whatever he denied now would only make him sound more guilty. "What was said?"

"Norris has put out word you're not to be trusted. He said you allowed gambling and drinking on site that caused one of your employees to get seriously hurt so you were let go."

Martin couldn't take a breath and his blood sounded too loud rushing in his ears. Connor was saying something else and Martin had to concentrate to hear him.

"Is any of that true?"

"No," said Martin. "But that doesn't make any difference, does it?"

"Afraid not, mate. You know how it is. I just can't take the risk because if the powers that be find out, I'll be shit-canned along with you."

"I understand, Connor." Martin felt like a heavy cloak was being draped over him and his mood was dropping with every moment.

"Sorry," said Connor and hung up.

Martin stared at his phone and tried to focus his thoughts. How many people had Norris managed to get to over the weekend? Even if they didn't believe Norris was telling the truth they would be in exactly the same position as Connor and wouldn't be able to take a chance. Accidents happen all the time and can sometimes be staged, and he wouldn't put it past Norris to do that.

So what could Martin do next? He couldn't continue to help Olivia financially if he didn't have any money coming in.

His phone rang and wrenched him out of his thoughts. Gordy's name showed on the display. "Hi."

"Hey, boss. I heard the news about Norris. I'm sorry you got dragged into it."

The apology sounded sincere, but it didn't do much to help him. "Yeah."

"Listen, man, I know it's my fault. I should have shut the card school down as soon as I found out about it but the chance to take Will for a few quid was too good a chance to pass up."

"Thirty grand isn't a few quid." Martin shook his head at the stupidity. "Surely you knew Will would tell Murray?"

"I didn't expect it to go like that. And that's the other thing, I wanted to thank you again for sticking up for me."

"I couldn't let them beat the shit out of you, Gordy. Even though I wanted to do it and still probably might if I get the chance."

Gordy chuckled without humour. "I get that and I deserve it."

"So what was the outcome for you?"

"Norris fucking owns me, doesn't he? He wants the full amount back with interest and if I don't meet my deadline then he'll have Sandy break my legs."

"Can you just give it to him?"

"You remember I got that new Mondeo the other week?"

"You really are an idiot, aren't you?"

"That's why I'm where I am and you're where you are. So he's got me doing shit duties at half pay and I don't stand a chance of paying him back. What did Jo say?"

"I haven't told her yet."

"You haven't…" There was a pause. "Fuck, Martin. What are you going to do?"

"I can't tell her. She knew about my gambling before and I promised her I was out of it. Even if she believes that, I still clobbered my boss." He let out a shaky breath. "I'll get it sorted."

"How? Your kid's at uni. Surely that's costing you, too."

Martin took a deep breath and looked out the window. People were making their way in and out of the shop, lost in their own worlds. He wondered how long it would be until he had to tell Jo they couldn't afford to go food shopping any more.

"I don't know, Gordy," he said. He felt sick. How could his world have collapsed so quickly? "I need to start earning."

"I can keep an eye out for jobs, if that helps. Or I might be able to help out with a bit of cash, too."

"How can you do that, if you're in the hole for thirty?"

"Because I know a man and plan to buy myself out of it. If you're interested, I can introduce you."

If Martin had been thinking rationally, he would have run a mile in the opposite direction. But all he could think about at that moment was how his world was closing in on itself. "That'd be good," he said. "Let me know when."

And that was Martin's third mistake.

Chapter 20

A shout woke Jo with a start.

It was light. Gayle's sleeping bag was empty. Jo rubbed her face and looked at her watch. It was just after seven.

The shout came again and it sounded like Tony. She heard running footsteps and then Peter shouted, "What is it?"

Jo got out of her sleeping bag, pulled on her boots and reached for her jacket but it wasn't where she'd left it. Confused, she lifted the rucksack up but it wasn't on the groundsheet, either. All she saw was Gayle's little coat, which didn't look large enough for Jo. She got out of the tent and stretched until her shoulders popped.

Sam was leaning on the end of his tent, hair askew and she could see now he had the makings of a bald patch. He was looking towards the cliff edge but seemed to be having trouble keeping his eyes open.

"Morning," she said and he shifted his attention to her. "You okay?"

"I'll live," he said. "I didn't sleep too well, I don't think." He rubbed his left eye. "How about you?"

"Like a log until someone started shouting."

"It's Tony. He's down by the cliff edge and seems to be getting a bit excited."

"I'll wander down," she said. "Have you seen Gayle?"

"I've only been out here since they started shouting. Isn't she in the tent with you?"

"No."

"Perhaps she's gone to the loo. I'll go and check." He gave her a half wave and turned towards the trees.

Jo walked around the tent. The sun was a glowing orb peering over the hills ahead and she looked away from the light. As she passed the firepit she saw the rain had turned the ashes into a black mush. She walked on and breathed in deeply. The crisp air felt almost restorative.

Tony and Martin were standing together looking over the edge. Peter was jogging toward them.

"Hey," she called. If he heard her, he didn't respond. "Hey, Peter!"

He stopped and cocked his head to one side like an inquisitive dog.

"Peter!" she called.

He turned and his mouth opened wide. "Jo?"

She gave him a confused shrug. "Who else was it likely to be?"

"Oh shit," he said and ran towards her. "You're okay?"

"Of course I am," she said. "Just a bit stiff from lying on the groundsheet." He looked worried, which only confused her more. "What's wrong?"

"I'm not too sure," he said with a vague shake of his head. He turned towards the edge and called Martin.

Her husband turned on his heel. She gave him a wave and then he was running towards her, his expression a mix of shock and happiness.

"Jo!" He ran into her and lifted her up and spun her around. He pulled her tight and kissed her hard on the lips then set her on her feet. "I don't understand." His eyes were rimmed red. "Where were you? I thought I'd lost you."

"How could you lose me when I was in the tent? What the hell's going on?"

Sam came up behind them. "She's not in the toilets."

"Oh shit," said Martin.

"Would somebody please tell me what's going on?" Jo demanded. "Is Gayle okay?"

Martin shook his head then took her hand and led her to the edge. Tony glanced over his shoulder and didn't bother to hide his surprise.

"Fuck me," he said.

Martin jumped down to the next level and held out a hand to help her down.

"I don't want to get too close to the edge."

"You need to," said Tony.

Martin lay down on the limestone and edged himself forward slowly. Tony lay beside him.

Peter stood beside her. His eyes seemed watery. "It's okay, Jo," he said and gestured for her to lie down.

Jo got to her knees, lowered herself gently onto her belly then wriggled until she could peek the edge. The ground, so far below, seemed to rush up and tilt at the same time and she closed her eyes until the wave of dizziness passed. She squinted her eyes open and glanced at Martin. "What am I looking for?"

"Down and to the left," said Martin and pointed.

With a deep breath, she looked again and saw something on a wide ledge far below her. It took her a moment to realise what it was. "Is someone down there?"

"Yes," said Martin.

The person was wearing hiking trousers and boots and a purple jacket that looked just like hers.

Jo's stomach rolled. "Oh no."

"What's going on, you lot?" asked Sam.

Jo pushed herself up and moved back until she came to the wall and sat with her back to it. Her stomach was turning somersaults. How could it possibly be Gayle down there? Even if she'd walked this far from the tent, she would have realised where she was when she fell over that first drop.

Peter sat Sam down and knelt in front of him. "We think we've found Gayle," he said.

"Great. Where is she?"

Tony glanced over his shoulder. "See for yourself."

"Fucking hell," Martin scolded him. "Have a heart, mate."

"What?" Tony sounded affronted.

"We think she's fallen over the cliff," said Peter gently.

"What're you talking about? She can't have." Sam quickly moved towards the edge.

"Lie here and look down," said Martin.

Sam did and his cry echoed out over the valley.

Jo pressed herself back against the rock.

Peter put a reassuring hand on her shoulder. "You're safe."

"How could she have fallen?" Jo asked. Her mind reeled. This didn't make any sense.

"What can we do?" asked Sam. There was a hitch in his voice and he roughly wiped away a tear.

"Not a lot," said Tony.

Martin pushed himself back from the edge and tried to pull Sam with him. The younger man resisted but then allowed himself to be moved and Martin put him against the rock beside Jo.

"We can't just leave her there," Sam said desperately.

Martin licked the corner of his mouth and Jo recognised the habit. He usually did it when he was deep in thought and trying to process the best course of action. "The lad's right, Peter," he said after a while. "We need to get some help up here."

"But how can we when there's no fucking signal?" said Sam plaintively. "I was trying all yesterday afternoon."

"We can use my satellite phone," Peter said. He cleared his throat. "I'll call the mountain rescue team. They'll come out straight away." He got to his feet as if the weight of the world were on his shoulders. "It's in my rucksack. I'll go and get it."

"I'll come with you," Jo said.

"Are you okay?" Martin asked her, his voice strained.

"No and I'll feel a lot safer when we're all away from that edge." She kissed him quickly on the cheek.

Peter helped her up onto the plateau and they crossed the grass towards the tents.

"We woke up last night," Jo said. "She said she was going to the latrine."

Peter shook his head ruefully. "I don't understand it at all. I've camped out here dozens of times, with all sorts of people, and nothing like this has ever happened before."

She touched his arm. "It wasn't your fault."

"I was in charge," he said slowly and wiped the corners of his mouth. "She was my responsibility."

"I understand that, Peter. But you gave us all warnings."

"Did you speak to her when she left your tent? Did she sound alert?"

"I'd have said so." She thought back to their conversation and what had woken her. "Actually, I heard someone else moving around the tent before she got up. I don't know who it was but maybe they saw her?"

"It's worth asking when we get back."

"So, what happens now?" Jo asked. It felt like she was walking through a dream.

"There's an emergency procedure that kicks in. I'll ring the mountain rescue and they'll scramble the proper response to recover Gayle."

His use of the word 'recover' made her pause and they walked around the firepit in silence. Then he said, "I didn't mean that tastelessly."

"I know."

"But the chances of her having survived are sadly very small."

"The ledge looks a long way down."

"It's about halfway I think, so well over one hundred feet."

She wondered when Gayle realised she was in the wrong place and the thought made her shudder. Would she have understood what was happening? How long did it take to fall a hundred feet or more and what would the poor young woman have been thinking in those long seconds?

Jo shook her head to try and dislodge that line of thinking, but it wouldn't go. If Gayle was alert and falling, then why didn't she scream?

"Did you hear anything weird last night?" she asked.

"When I take my hearing aids out of a night-time, Jo, you could drop a bomb next to me and I might not hear it. Why?"

"I was just thinking about Gayle falling."

"Please don't. You'll only drive yourself mad."

"I can't help it. Even if she fell over the edge then why didn't she scream or shout out?"

"Perhaps she didn't wake up properly," he said with tenderness, although she couldn't work out if that was for his or her benefit. "Maybe she stumbled and fell and knocked her head. It was probably all over in seconds."

She was sure he was right, but something didn't make sense to her and she couldn't believe, in the stillness of the night, that nobody had heard anything.

"The first I knew about it was Martin shouting," Peter said. "I ran over and when I saw the body wearing your jacket, I understood his terror."

"That must have been horribly frightening," she said. It hadn't occurred to her just how scared Martin must have been before he saw her.

"Why was she wearing your jacket?"

"She must have picked it up by mistake in the dark."

She stopped beside his tent as he grabbed his rucksack. He opened one of the side pockets and felt inside it. He frowned and checked another pocket.

"That's odd," he muttered. He opened the top of the pack and reached in. "I can't find it."

"Are you sure you packed it?"

"Of course I did." He gave her a stern glance. "It's part of the checklist I go through with Ross every time we start a hike. I always keep it in the side pocket, for easy access." He searched through the pack again. "Shit, where is it?"

"Is it a big phone? Could it have got caught up in something?"

Peter knelt down and upended his rucksack on the groundsheet. There were a handful of clothes rolled up into tight tubes, a peaked cap, several ration packs, some protein bars and two bottles of water.

"It's not here," he said, but didn't sound as though he believed himself. He re-checked the side pockets and even held them up for Jo to inspect but they were empty. "Where the bloody hell is it?"

"You didn't take it out for any reason?"

"There's no reason to. It's not a smartphone, all it does is ring." He pushed the rucksack away. "Shit."

"Now what?"

"Now we're going to have to come up with a plan B."

"You don't already have one?"

"Never needed one," he said and got up. She heard his knees pop. "Come on."

He stalked across the grass and she kept pace but when he abruptly stopped she bumped into him.

"Sorry," she said.

Peter waved her apology off. "Look." He pointed towards the firepit. "There."

She looked at the mushy ashes and the pot with a growing sense of exasperation. "I don't know what you're looking at, Peter."

"The earth's wet."

"It rained."

"I know it did. But look at the earth by the stones."

Footprints described a route around the firepit and were mostly imprinted over one another, as if each walker had followed almost the same trail. But off to the right of the stones was a set of smudged footprints with two grooves running between them.

"What am I looking at?" she asked.

"I think those grooves come from someone being dragged." Peter turned and slowly made his way back towards the tents.

"I thought we were going to work on plan B?" she called after him.

He held up a finger then stopped and pointed at the ground again. "Come and look."

She walked over to join him and saw a disturbed area of mud between the tents and the treeline.

"There was a scuffle here," he said.

"How can you tell? All I can see are footprints."

"No, the ground is churned. Footprints, even when people tread where someone else already has been, leave ridges. A scuffle is messier, you see? That's not people stepping, that's feet dragging."

"Are you serious?"

"Look at it," he said urgently. "This is pretty much in line with your tent, which makes sense if Gayle was heading to the latrines." He looked back towards the three men at the edge. "I know I didn't leave my tent overnight. Did you?"

"No," she said, feeling a ripple of gooseflesh run down her arms as realisation dawned.

"The footprints and scuffle and grooves must have something to do with Gayle. You said you heard someone before she woke up, didn't you? Well, I don't think she was on her own when she came out for a wee last night, Jo."

"You think someone dragged her to the edge and pushed her over?"

"I don't understand it but that's what it looks like to me." He put a hand on her arm. "I've just had another horrible thought and I don't want to worry you, but I feel like I should say it."

"What?"

"Gayle came out of your tent wearing your jacket."

Chapter 21

Martin, Five Weeks Ago

The Spot-On snooker club on Montagu Street looked like it hadn't been updated since the eighties and a portrait of Steve Davis looked down on them as Martin followed Gordy upstairs.

The hall was a large, murky room that smelled of onions, rancid cooking oil and body odour. Three of the tables were occupied and the lights above the greens looked pale and sickly. The windows were all covered with black plastic.

Martin knew he was making a mistake but couldn't see any other way out. Everyone, it seemed, had heard about the blackballing and he had no other viable way of raising money.

"This is your last chance to turn around," Gordy said.

"I can't. Olivia facetimed us last night about a trip that would be really useful for her course." It was a fortnight in Berlin giving her on-the-job training and valuable experience, but it cost five thousand pounds. "She's working every shift McDonald's will give her but there's no way she could afford it. Jo agreed to help her out."

"You still haven't told her?"

Martin shook his head. "That moment's passed. I need the money."

"I understand but this is a big deal, Martin. Tommy McLain doesn't work for HSBC or NatWest."

"I'm not an idiot, Gordy. They wouldn't help me anyway."

"Did you even ask them?"

"Of course I did." The phone calls had been painful and embarrassing as the banks pointed out his past reckless behaviour still hindered him. "They're not interested."

"I'm trying to warn you because you're not as streetwise as you like to think you are. If you don't honour the terms with Mr McLain then you won't be getting polite letters or term arrangements to pay off the money. You'll have to pay it come what may."

"And I will."

"I don't think you properly understand, but if you're sure," said Gordy.

He led them to the bar. A bored-looking woman with bleached blonde hair stood behind the counter wiping a glass over with a cloth that looked like it should be burned. She barely gave them a glance. Off to one side of the counter was a door marked 'private'. Gordy stood in front of it and raised his hand.

The door opened before he could knock and a tall thin man with very closely cropped white hair glared at Gordy and then at Martin. "You haven't got an appointment, Gordy."

"I know, Sandy. But we want to see Mr McLain."

Sandy's lip twitched as he gave a little shrug. "I got to ask." He closed the door then opened it again a few moments later. "Come on."

They went into a long, narrow room with a wide desk at the far end. A large window behind it looked out over Hadlington. A man in a suit with thinning grey hair sat behind the desk. He was on a landline phone and waved Gordy and Martin to seats in front of the desk. Sandy sat at a chair by the door and picked up a newspaper.

Martin sat down. The man on the phone mimicked someone talking and smiled then made a circular motion with a finger as if he wanted the other person to hurry up. It was a couple of minutes before he put the phone down.

"Gordy," he said. "Long time no see. I'd ask if life was treating you better these days but, if it was, you wouldn't be here, would you?"

"No, Mr McLain. Things have been on the up for the past few months because I've been working with Martin here." He jerked his thumb towards Martin. "We had a decent job and it was good money but I got stupid."

"I heard." McLain fixed his attention on Martin and leaned forward, knitting his fingers together. "I take it you're Martin Harper?"

"I am."

He leaned to one side so he could see around Martin. "We've heard of Martin Harper, haven't we, Sandy?"

"We have," confirmed Sandy.

"So what can I do for you, Martin?" McLain asked, focussing his attention on him. "Are you looking for a job?"

Martin hadn't considered a job in a pool hall but decided beggars couldn't be choosers. "If you have one?"

McLain laughed like he'd just heard the best joke in the world ever. When he calmed down, he coughed. "I have a few. Is that what you need?"

"We're interested in a couple of loans, Mr McLain," said Gordy.

"Really? Well you're a bit naughty coming here direct and you know it. If I wasn't feeling in such a good mood today, I'd have Sandy take you outside and remind you of the rules."

Martin glanced at Gordy who looked worried. "I'm sorry, Mr McLain," Gordy said. "I should have gone to see…"

McLain held up his hand with a benevolent smile. "No, you're here now. But we'll count that as strike one, shall we?"

Martin looked from Gordy to Mr McLain and the tension between them was almost palpable.

"So, is it you that needs the loan, Gordy?"

"No, it's the pair of us."

McLain seemed amused. "Are you setting up home or something?"

"No," said Martin. He felt a chill just looking at McLain and wanted to get up and walk away. His throat felt suddenly dry. Nothing good was going to come of this.

McLain put his elbows on the desk and steepled his fingers. "I don't think this is your world, Martin, but I'm willing to give you a chance because you seem like a decent bloke. How much do you want?"

Martin had spent an anguished few hours working through the figures and taking into account Jo's salary, their joint savings and the assumption that he'd be able to find something else soon. It was depressing and frightening and made the assumption that Jo would never find out. But the very fact she controlled the household expenses meant that, very soon, she'd know he'd been lying to her about his gambling from almost as soon as they'd met. "I would need ten thousand," he said.

McLain made a moue face and nodded his head. "How about you, Gordy?"

"The same."

McLain leaned back in his chair and the leather creaked under him. "We can do that," he said.

"Thank you," said Gordy.

"Yes, thanks, Mr McLain," said Martin.

"And yet neither of you know my terms yet." He leaned forward and tapped some keys on a desktop calculator. "So ten grand with compound interest and no bonus for early repayment." McLain smiled at his own joke and then quoted the figure.

It took Martin's breath away and would almost double his debt but what choice did he have? "That's a bit higher than I was expecting."

"Well, that's disappointing," said McLean and he leaned over to one side again. "He said that's a bit higher than he was expecting, Sandy."

Sandy laughed loudly.

McLain righted himself in the chair. "Maybe you've never dealt with anything like this before so let me explain how it works. You came to me, I didn't advertise. Since it's my money I'm lending then I need to make something out of it as well as protect my investment. I'm sure you understand that. On the other hand, you're welcome to walk away and we'll still be friends." McLain smiled and there was absolutely no warmth in it at all. "What do you say?"

Martin bit the inside of his lip. It didn't make sense but where else was he going to get the money without revealing he still gambled? "Okay," he said.

"Good," said McLain. "Now Gordy can take you to my associate who will sort all of this out because no transactions are done in my office." He leaned forward again. "But if you're seriously looking for a job to tide you over, I might have something."

Chapter 22

"Peter thinks what?" Martin's voice dripped with incredulity. "How much did he drink last night?"

Once Jo got back to the edge, she pulled Martin to one side and then led him back to the firepit, leaving the others there.

"Not as much as me," she said. "I know it doesn't make any sense but look at the tracks."

Martin saw the tracks straight away and his intake of breath was audible. She stepped closer and was going to hug him, but he made no move to let her. She stroked her bracelet instead.

"They could have been made by anything," he said but didn't sound convinced. He rubbed the side of his head.

"Or by someone dragging Gayle," she said. "Look, you can see them all the way to the rock."

"But why would someone do that? The only person who knew her before yesterday morning was Sam."

"What if they weren't looking for Gayle? She was wearing my jacket. You thought it was me."

"Why would anyone be after you?" She saw a flash of anger in his eyes. "Does that old bastard think I wanted to hurt you?"

"No, I don't think he meant that at all."

"What else could he mean? I was the only person here who knew you before yesterday morning."

"Perhaps they weren't looking for me or her specifically, but she just happened to leave the tent at the wrong moment."

"So, he's saying any one of us could be a random killer, waiting for someone to pop out of their tent?"

"I don't know, Martin."

"Well, that's what it sounds like. Does that mean it's one of us, including him or is he including that bald man Tony saw yesterday?"

"Who none of the rest of us saw," she pointed out.

Martin paused. "Do you think he was lying?" he asked curiously.

"I wouldn't say that directly but nobody else saw the mystery man. And I still can't put my finger on why Tony seems familiar."

"There's a big difference between finding someone familiar and them being a killer." He walked back towards the edge, keeping his eyes on the grooves in the dirt. Jo followed him. "It doesn't make any sense at all, Jo, unless we assume Sam felt humiliated by Gayle last night and lay in wait for her? Even though she was wearing your jacket, he could probably see her face."

"He was sloshed last night."

"He might have been acting." Martin shook his head. "It feels like we're jumping to conclusions. Why are you so sure this wasn't just some terrible, tragic accident?"

"Because the evidence is there."

Martin went to say something then stopped and licked the side of his mouth. When he reached the path, he glanced around the plateau. "You do realise if you and Peter are right then it means someone up here with us now is the killer."

Peter came along the path towards them. "Okay, folks," he said. "We have a problem."

"I'd say so," said Sam. He'd regained some of his composure though his eyes were still red.

"I mean, I can't find my satellite phone. It was secured in one of the side pockets of my rucksack when we left Hadley Hall yesterday but it's no longer there. Both Jo and I checked and I've now searched all over and it's not here. It's bright yellow, so it's not like it's hiding in plain sight."

"So where the fuck is it?" asked Tony. "And what do we do now that we don't have it?"

Sam took out his phone and held it above his head. "Nothing," he muttered. "Not even one bar."

"I do have a contingency plan," said Peter.

"I'm sure you do," said Martin. "Does this involve you unmasking who deliberately hurt Gayle?"

Sam looked at him. "What did you say?"

"Don't," said Jo. Peter looked at her sadly and she shrugged – what-could-I-do? "Martin, we don't–"

"No, we need to get this out in the open. Peter has reason to believe Gayle was manhandled last night."

"He didn't say that," Jo said.

"What's going on?" Tony asked. He had spots of angry colour in his cheeks. "If I'm out of contact with the rest of the world in the middle of nowhere and stuck in the company of a murderer, then you'd better bloody well tell me."

"I didn't say that," said Peter and sounded as if he was struggling to maintain a steady tone. "I observed that from the footprints and the grooves it looks like Gayle wasn't alone last night."

"The ground's soaked and we've all churned it up this morning." Tony looked from Sam to Martin. "And if you're trying to cast blame, I didn't know any of you from Adam before yesterday. But if something did happen to Gayle, I suggest we look at Lanky Lad here."

"Hey," Sam protested. His voice hitched and he bit his lip.

"That's enough," said Peter sharply. "We don't know what happened but we need to check on Gayle, so let's focus on that."

Tony made a dismissive sound. "She's on a ledge a hundred feet or more down. I can't see her climbing up and none of us are going to climb down so I say we have to go and get help."

"I can check her," said Peter.

"How?" Martin asked. "Can you fly?"

"No, but like I said to you before, I've climbed this face. There'll be pitons left from the climbing groups and there's rope in the brick store. If we rig something up, you could lower me down."

"That's bloody idiotic," said Tony. "I say we go straight to the hotel. We could be there within a couple of hours."

"We can't leave Gayle," protested Sam.

"Why not?" Tony asked. "We can't do much for her."

"Are you trying to be horrible?" Jo asked him. "Or does it just come naturally?"

He gave her a look. "I'm trying to be realistic."

"I'd feel better if we just checked," said Peter.

"So would I," said Sam.

"And me," Jo said.

Everyone looked at Martin.

"I happen to think Tony's right," Martin said, "but if you're all adamant and Peter reckons he can do it, then we should give it a try."

"Why don't I go and get the rope from the brick store?" Jo asked. "We need to try and be safe."

"Good thinking," said Martin.

Jo walked towards the firepit and found her eyes drawn to the grooves in the earth. She was perhaps a dozen or so steps from the edge when she heard Martin shout, "No!"

She turned quickly, fearing the worst. Silhouetted by the sun, he had his hands on his head and then ducked out of sight.

"Shit," she said. "What now?"

Chapter 23

Jo ran for the step.

Martin had stopped shouting and she had the horrible feeling he'd somehow gone over the edge too. Her heart was pounding by the time they reached the edge.

Tony was lying on his belly and looking into the drop. Martin was crouched beside him and the sense of relief she felt made her lightheaded for a moment. Sam knelt behind the two men.

"What's happened?" Jo asked.

Martin glanced over his shoulder. "Peter's gone over."

"What?" she said even though she'd heard him perfectly. What the hell was going on?

"One minute he was talking about Gayle and then he fell."

"Is he dead?" Sam asked.

"No," said Tony and rolled onto his side. "He's on the next ledge down, about six or eight feet. One leg's twisted weird and he's not moving much."

"This is fucking insane," said Martin.

"He just pitched forward like he was diving into a pool," said Tony. He sounded winded. "He didn't scream or yell and I thought he was gone until I heard him groaning."

Even though she'd done it once before, Jo still found it overwhelming to lay herself down next to Martin and peer over the edge. She wriggled forward and the ground seemed an impossible distance away. Her stomach rolled. Martin held the waistband of her trousers.

"I've got you," he said.

She edged forward until she could see Peter on a narrow ledge a few feet below. His leg was at an odd angle and had to be broken. "Peter?" she called.

"He's probably unconscious," said Martin.

"We have to help him," said Jo.

"Are you going to climb down and bring him back?" asked Tony sarcastically.

Even the thought of it made her feel ill. "I can't. But one of us will have to because he's the only person who knows where we're heading."

"I can read a map," said Tony. "I've got one on my phone."

"It won't work," said Sam.

"Of course it will. We've got GPS, haven't we?"

"Yes," said Sam and sounded like he was trying to explain something to a five-year-old. "But if we haven't got a signal, even if you use the map embedded in the phone, all you'll see is a big green shape for the national park and, if you're lucky, an arrow somewhere in the middle of it."

"I'll climb down," said Martin.

"Let me get the rope then. We need to make sure you're safe."

"We haven't got time," Martin said. "What if he falls?"

"What if you do?" she demanded.

Martin didn't say anything but quickly shimmied to the edge, turned and levered himself over. He tipped Jo a wink and she wanted to wish him luck, but her heart was in her throat and she couldn't speak. Martin dropped out of sight and she pressed herself against the rock as her mind conjured images of him standing on that horribly narrow ledge. If he lost his balance…

"He's on the ledge," Sam said. "He's helping Peter to his feet. The old boy is hopping and Martin's trying to get him to stop."

"Please don't tell me that," said Jo. She could picture Peter hopping and Martin grabbing him and gravity pulling them over.

"It's okay, he's up. Tony, grab his other arm."

The two men pulled Peter up and the old man's face was contorted in agony. Jo helped Tony pull him away from the edge then knelt beside Peter while the others helped Martin up.

Peter's broken leg moved like a toy doll's. She tried not to pay it too much attention.

"Hey," she said.

He had a big graze on his forehead and his eyes were unfocussed. He moved his lips but didn't speak.

"Peter? It's Jo. Can you hear me?"

He nodded gently and winced. "Yeah," he murmured.

"What happened? Did you fall?"

Peter shook his head with the barest of movements. "Don't know." He licked his lips. "No."

Had she heard him properly? She leaned in. "Did someone push you?"

Martin knelt on the other side of Peter's head. "I'm afraid I only know the basics of first aid," he said. "Does anywhere else hurt apart from your leg?"

"My leg doesn't hurt," Peter said. "My head does though. It's thumping and I feel sick."

"You're probably concussed," Martin said. "We need to get you back. Do you have the map?"

"It's in my pocket."

Martin nodded at Jo and she checked delicately through Peter's pockets until she found the folded map.

"Now what?" asked Tony.

Everyone looked at everyone else. "We need a plan," she said and looked at Martin.

"Here's what I think we ought to do," Martin said, "but if anyone has a better idea then please chip in. I reckon we try to figure out where the farm with the free-range eggs is and get Peter there."

"Smith," said Peter.

"Who's Smith?" Jo asked.

"Smith's at the farm. Keep going past the trees. You can't miss it."

"We'll find it, thank you," said Martin. "I suggest we make some kind of stretcher for Peter and then get him to the farm. We can ring the mountain rescue people from there."

"And how do we make a stretcher?" asked Tony.

They all looked at one another and then Sam took a deep breath. "We can do it with a couple of long, strong sticks," he said. "I did it in the scouts. We use the sticks as handles and then thread them through the arms of a couple of jackets."

"Oh," said Tony mockingly. "It's that easy, is it?"

"Sounds easy enough to me," said Jo.

"I think that might work," said Martin. "We'll go and find the sticks." He looked from Sam to Tony. "But keep well away from each other, just in case."

"Yeah," said Tony. "I don't want to be in the trees with Killer here."

"What did you call me?" Sam demanded.

"Kidder. You know, a big kid." Tony smiled sarcastically at Sam.

Sam scowled. "You're an arse, Tony."

Martin turned to Jo. "Did you want to stay here with Peter, Jo?"

"I can collect sticks, too," she said.

"I know, but someone needs to stay with Peter."

"And that's a girl's job, is it?"

"No," he said and gripped her hand tightly for a moment. She met his gaze and saw something in his eyes that might have been pain or fear.

"Okay."

The three men walked off towards the wood keeping a good distance between each other.

"Why are they leaving you alone?" Peter asked.

Jo squatted beside him. "They're going to get some sticks to make a stretcher."

"Shouldn't be alone," he said. "You need to be careful."

"Why would any of them want to hurt me?"

He glared at her with the intensity of a prophet or a madman. "Because you're here with them. And you know what they've done."

"So do you."

"Yes. I think we're both in danger."

He closed his eyes.

If he was concussed, was that confusing him? If it wasn't, then she had to accept he was right and they were in danger. As much as she couldn't believe it was Martin, one of these men was a killer. And she was trapped on a moor with him.

Chapter 24

Sam came back first with a long branch and a spare jacket over his shoulder.

"How is he?" he asked quietly.

"Sleeping, I think."

"No," muttered Peter without opening his eyes. "I'm doing a solo from Swan Lake."

Sam frowned. "What the hell does that mean?"

"He's concussed but has a good sense of humour."

"Oh," said Sam. "Are you okay for me to sit next to you, or would you rather I sat somewhere else?"

He looked hurt and confused.

"Sit next to me," Jo said.

He sat with his knees to his chest and his elbows resting on them.

"How are you feeling?" Jo asked.

"Shitty." He unconsciously brushed his hair back over his bald spot, but a breeze lifted it off a moment or two later. "There was so much to her that people couldn't see or didn't want to. They saw her hair and eyebrows and career choice and dismissed her as a bimbo but that wasn't her at all."

"We had a bit of a talk yesterday and I thought she was lovely."

"She was." He looked at her. "What do I do now? I mean, how can she be dead? How am I supposed to feel?"

Was it possible he'd never experienced grief before? "How you feel is how you should feel, Sam. She was a good friend of yours. It's going to hurt." Jo wondered if Gayle had managed to speak to him about how she felt but knew it would be too upsetting to ask.

"I feel kind of empty, like this is all a horrible dream."

"That's a normal reaction."

"I'm also struggling with whether to film this or not."

He said it so blandly, like a man curious about what was for dinner, that it took Jo a moment to properly understand him. "Film what?"

"This," Sam said and spread his arms wide. "Something bad happened here and we need to find the answers. I'm a YouTuber with a camera, I have a very personal connection and I'm on the scene. Why shouldn't I be

115

filming?" He smiled sadly. "It's what Gayle would have wanted," he said quietly.

It sounded horribly ghoulish to her. "Are you joking?"

"No. She'd have wanted me to document it because it's what I do. What if Peter's right and one of us is the killer? News programmes will want footage and I might capture the truth because I'm here."

Her disgust at his detachment was growing. "I can't believe…"

"I'm not being horrible," he said. "I'd want her to do the same thing if I'd fallen."

His excuses sounded to Jo like he was trying a new role on for size as the victim's partner. Even if he was right about the authorities wanting on-the-spot images, this felt horribly exploitative.

What if he were the killer? She'd seen those people who went to press conferences crying and pleading for answers when, all the time, they were the cause of the anguish. Was all this an act? Was he really sitting next to her feeling hurt and vulnerable or was he acting the part?

"What about Peter? Did you see what happened with him?"

"No. I was looking the other way and then Martin was shouting and I couldn't believe it."

Martin came back carrying two thick poles. Tony wasn't far behind him and had a jacket draped over one shoulder.

"How is he?" asked Martin.

"It's almost like he's dozing," Jo said. "I don't understand how he's not in agony."

"Well let's get him moved before he does start to feel stuff," Martin said.

"What the fuck are you doing?" demanded Tony.

Jo glanced at Sam who was filming their discussion. "He's getting footage for when we get back," she explained.

Martin pulled a face. "That's not on, mate."

"It's fucking sick is what it is," Tony said. "What're you going to do? Put it on YouTube so you can make some dosh off your bird?"

"No," said Sam defensively.

"Then put the fucking thing away," said Tony and watched Sam until he switched the camera off. As he laid it down, Jo noticed he'd turned the unit so the lens faced them.

"So how do we do it?" Jo asked.

Sam gave his spare jacket to her. "Zip it up then turn it inside out." She did as he instructed. "You do the same, Tony."

Martin handed Sam the two poles. They were smooth and solid-looking lengths of wood. "They were leaning against the brick store, I think someone had broken down a fence somewhere."

Sam looked at his own branch and then threw it over the cliff. "Right, if you feed the poles through the arms on the inside…"

Within a couple of minutes they had a makeshift contraption that looked like a stretcher.

"Credit where it's due," said Martin. "You've done a good job there, Sam."

"Thanks."

"So now what?" Jo asked.

"Lay it next to Peter," Martin said.

He picked up one end and Tony took the other. Sam moved out of their way and now filmed them openly. Neither man seemed to notice. They put the stretcher down on Peter's right.

"Now we need to lift him," said Martin and looked at Jo.

"How do we do that without hurting him?" she asked.

"We don't," said Martin. He leaned over and put his hand on the older man's chest. "Hey, Peter. We're going to put you on the stretcher and we'll be as careful as we can but it's going to hurt like a bastard."

Peter opened his eyes. "I understand."

All four of them helped and the moment they lifted Peter off the ground he screamed so loud Jo almost let go of him to cover her ears. The sound ricocheted around her and, in the panic, they almost flung him onto the stretcher.

Peter stopped screaming and his cheeks glistened with tears.

"Sorry," said Martin.

"It's done," Peter said through gritted teeth. "I'm sorry I screamed."

"I think I'd have screamed louder than that," Martin said, then looked at Tony. "Your turn to shine," he said. "Get us to that farm."

Tony unfolded the Ordnance Survey Map and laid it out on the rock.

"The four 'X' marks are the car park, Irchester Flow, the farm and the hotel," said Peter. He shifted on the stretcher but the effort made him grimace. "It's for safety so if anything happens to me you can find your way back."

"I can do this, said Tony.

"Sure you can," said Martin. "Me and Jo will take the poles at the head, you two take the feet."

* * *

Manoeuvring the stretcher without hurting their patient proved to be harder than Jo had expected. Before they left, she went through Peter's pack and gave him a couple of paracetamol tablets. It was unlikely they'd be much help but even if they only took the edge off his pain that would be good. As it was, every misstep or trip seemed to be magnified through the bearers' arms and even though Peter held it together well he still let out the occasional whimper. She couldn't imagine how much pain he was in.

They rested at the edge of the plateau where ridges in the earth formed rough steps down onto the moor. A thin sheet of sweat coated her brow and upper lip and her T-shirt stuck to her back.

"This is hard work," she said.

Tony and Sam muttered their agreement. Martin didn't say anything.

The hill swept up to her left beyond the woods and the top of the valley seemed a long way above them. The incline to the right seemed very steep. None of the routes looked easy to negotiate with the stretcher.

Tony consulted the map. "We go straight by the woods then keep bearing left," he said. "The farm looks like it's right on the edge of the MoD land."

"Let's just hope they've got a phone," Jo said.

Chapter 25

Martin, Three Weeks Ago

Martin still hadn't found a company willing to take him on in the two weeks since he arranged the loan. He'd gone through every contact in his phone and even dug out a couple of black books from the loft but nobody could help. The only solid lead he'd had was for an installation supervisor in Northern France, which would have been virtually impossible to explain away to Jo and then he discovered it would pay less than he was making driving for Tommy McLain.

There was no way he could make the payment as things stood and the stress of that realisation weighed heavily on him. His appetite for everything faded and he didn't sleep more than a handful of hours a night, so his frayed nerves meant he was snappy at the best of times. Jo didn't seem comfortable with him either, and the only bright spot was seeing Olivia's grateful delight at the Berlin trip.

* * *

Jo was in the kitchen making dinner when he got home. Martin hung up his coat then checked the post she'd put on the table. A few bills and something from their insurance company.

'Shit,' he thought. 'Surely we don't have to renew anything yet?'

He left the bills alone and opened the insurance letter. It was a confirmation request for their life assurance policy as to whom the funds should be left to.

Breathing a sigh of relief, he went into the kitchen. "Hey," he said.

"Hey." Normally she would purse her lips for a kiss but today she didn't look away from stirring the bubbling bolognese sauce. Her body language spoke volumes.

"Is everything okay?" Had she found out about his lie? Did someone see him in the van and tell her?

"Not really. Some wanker clipped my car and drove off without leaving a note."

"Is it damaged?" he asked. He was relieved that was the reason but hoped he sounded concerned.

"Yes," she said with venom. "They whacked into the wing and dented it enough that the bodywork pushed into the tyre. I had to get the AA to tow the car to the garage."

He felt a chill as if someone had thrown cold water down his back. "You put it into the garage?"

"What did you expect me to do? I couldn't drive it as it was and I need it for work."

"Shit." A crocked car meant money.

"I know. The bastard could have at least left a note. They smacked it so hard there's no way they could have done it and not bloody noticed."

He felt his stress level rise sharply and leaned against the countertop.

"Aren't you going to say anything?" she asked angrily.

"What do you want me to say?" he asked and as soon as the words were out of his mouth, he knew he'd made a mistake.

"Seriously? Jesus, Martin, I know you've been distracted for the past few weeks, but you could at least take a little bit of interest in my life."

"I am interested in your life," he said but knew it was too little too late.

"Maybe you should show it a little more often then."

"Jo," he said and touched her arm.

She shrugged him off. "No, don't bother. Dinner won't be long, so get the wine out."

He uncorked a bottle from the rack and reached over her shoulder to take a couple of glasses out the cupboard. He accidentally nudged her elbow and she sighed.

"I'm sorry if it sounded like I wasn't interested," he said. "I've just got a lot of things on my mind."

"I'd noticed," she said and rested the wooden spoon against the frying pan. "That's been the case for a while, hasn't it?" She brushed her palms together. "Is something going on?"

'Oh shit,' he thought, 'she does know.' "What do you mean?"

"With us. With you," she clarified. "Are you seeing someone?"

"What?" He felt insulted.

"Is there someone else?"

"No," he said, letting the offence sound in his voice. If he threw this back at her it might give him a chance to think of a way out. He hated himself for the casual cruelty but couldn't see any other way to deal with it. "Of course not. Why would you think that?"

Jo bit the inside of her cheek then took a deep breath and let it out slowly. "I'm sorry, Martin, but everything's got on top of me today. First the car and then this constant worry about you."

"Why are you worried about me?"

"Because you've been so distant recently it's almost like I don't exist."

"Oh, sweetheart," he said. "That's not true at all and I wouldn't cheat on you." He hadn't intended to freeze her out but that must have been how it seemed, with his mind so completely focussed on getting himself out of this hole. Why hadn't he just told her on that first night?

"I know but it seemed like you've been struggling with something you really wanted to tell me but couldn't find a way."

The pang in his chest hit again. "It's my fault." The hurt in her eyes was painful to see. "Work's been really shitty and I got so wrapped up in it I let myself get distracted."

"You know you can talk to me, though. We're a team."

"I know." He pulled her into a hug. "I'm a shitty husband."

"Not all the time," she said. "Just when you ignore me and don't get annoyed my car got hit."

The reminder of the bill was a cold finger stroking the back of his neck. "I'm sorry. I'll make it up to you."

"Just tell me everything'll be fine."

"Of course it will," he said, glad that he wasn't facing her so she could see into his eyes. "You don't have anything to worry about."

She nodded as best she could in the embrace. "Good. I hope you get everything at work sorted out soon so I get my husband back."

"Me too," he said.

* * *

Gordy rang as Martin was loading the dishwasher. Jo was in the lounge checking her phone.

"Hey, boss. How's it going?"

"Like I'm swimming in a river of shit. How about you?"

"The same. I was assembling I-beam today and got burned on the rivet gun."

"Oh." It was hard to generate sympathy since Gordy was the reason they were both in such a mess.

"Any luck with the job hunt?"

"Nope."

"Fuck. Did you want to grab a drink tonight? We can talk strategy if you want."

"If you have a strategy for dealing with Tommy McLain then I would love to hear it."

"I'll meet you in the Sun at eight."

* * *

The Rising Sun pub was an old three-storey building with a squeaky sign and two big windows on either side of the door. Martin hadn't been in for a few years but it looked exactly as he remembered it.

The small dining area was empty and half a dozen old men sat at the horseshoe-shaped bar. Beyond it were a series of booths. One was occupied by a handful of women playing Scrabble. Gordy was sitting a couple of booths away and two pints were on the table in front of him. He raised his hand in greeting as Martin walked over.

"Evening, boss. I got you a pint."

"Cheers," said Martin as he sat down.

Gordy held up his hand. "Look at this bastard." The burn was about an inch wide and three inches long and the skin was red and rippled. "I haven't been burned on the job in years."

Martin still couldn't generate any sympathy. "Well, if you hadn't been so keen to rip off Will Norris, neither of us would be in this position."

"Alright, alright." Gordy picked at a beer mat. "You're a bit peaky today, aren't you?"

"Are you surprised? I found out tonight my wife thinks I'm having an affair but all I can focus on is that I can't cover the loan. I'm shitting myself about it, frankly, because Olivia's trip took out a big chunk, and what I'm getting paid driving the van doesn't even scratch the surface."

"Same here."

"So, what happens if we can't afford to pay McLain back? You had money off him before. Did you pay it all back on time?"

"Nope." Gordy stared intently at the beer mat. "I needed an extra week and when I told Sandy he gave me a reminder."

"Did you beat you up?"

Gordy chuckled without mirth. "No, because bruises fade pretty quickly." He held up his right hand. The upper joint of his little finger was bent at an angle to the knuckle. "You remember I said I broke this on a job once? Well, I didn't. Sandy said I needed to take my responsibilities seriously and if I didn't come up with the full amount by the next week, with additional interest, naturally, he was going for my knee."

"Shit." Martin's stomach lurched and he thought, for a moment, he was going to be sick. He couldn't imagine the pain of someone breaking his finger or, worse, trying to shatter his kneecap.

"Would you be able to meet the payment if you told Jo about it now?"

"Not unless we sell the house. The only thing I have to my name otherwise is life assurance."

"That's not going to help. If you die, Mr McLain will still go after his debt to be repaid."

Martin retched and swallowed back the bile. "This is fucking terrible, Gordy."

"I know." Gordy drank some of his pint then put the glass on the table carefully. "I do have another idea though."

Martin wiped the corners of his mouth with his thumb and forefinger. "If it's as bright as the one about getting a loan then I'll pass."

"It's better than that."

"Does it involve robbing a bank?"

"Not quite," said Gordy. He rolled his shoulders until something clicked. "You said before that you'd once been a gambling man."

"I was but not anymore."

"Would you be willing to change for a sure thing?"

"Sure things don't really exist," said Martin.

"But what if one did?" Gordy leaned forward conspiratorially as if the Scrabble players might be eavesdropping. "I know a man."

Martin stood up in a flash of anger. "Fucking hell, Gordy. You said you had a strategy."

"I do, boss. Sit down, please, it's a plan and it's a good one. My mate Hughie works at the Body Plant gym in town." Gordy gestured for Martin to sit down. "He's one of the trainers and he's got a boxer called Rick Browne who's apparently going to be the next Rocky Balboa. The kid's got a right hand like an anvil and he has a fight on Friday evening."

"Betting on a boxing match sounds almost as bad as going to a loan shark to tide us over."

"But Hughie says the kid is solid gold and the card's been announced. His opponent is so far over the hill he's almost out of sight."

Alarm bells were ringing but Gordy seemed convinced. "How can we be sure your mate Hughie is telling the truth?" Martin asked.

Gordy sat back. "We can't, Martin, okay? I've known him for years and he's a straight arrow but I can't guarantee anything. If we take this chance, though, and it pays off, then our worries are solved."

"And if it doesn't, we're back to square one with less money."

"If we don't pay up in a fortnight it won't matter if we're a penny shy or have no cash at all, we're fucked."

Martin felt the bile rise again. "Where's this tournament?"

"Out at Kilburn Farm."

The location didn't ease his worry. "A tournament at a farm?"

"It's an underground thing, very few rules and shit like that. But there's a lot of betting there. Hughie took me to one a few months back and the cash floating around was incredible. Blokes driving Beamers and Mercs and flashing wads of notes as they watched these poor kids knock seven shades of shit out of each other. If we go in and bet heavy on Rick, we could clean up. What do you think, boss?"

It sounded like a terrible idea, but Martin couldn't think of a better one. "How much do you have left to put on?" he asked.

Chapter 26

The farm wasn't as close as Tony said and even though Peter wasn't a heavy man, the pressure in Jo's arms increased with every step. The rough texture of the pole felt like it was rubbing her palm and fingers raw and Tony reminded them all he'd skinned his palms yesterday on the Devil's Steps. Sam moaned about his aching arms and legs to the extent Jo wished he'd just shut up, and he clearly wasn't endearing himself to the other men. Peter flitted in and out of a doze but when he seemed fully awake, he was in a lot of pain.

"Is that it over there?" Martin asked.

She looked over the trees and caught glimpses of what looked like a white building.

"It must be," said Tony. "Bank up towards it."

"How come we seem to be walking uphill constantly?" Sam asked.

"Are you blaming me for it?" Tony demanded.

"Not unless you're reading the map wrong."

"For fuck's sake, you lanky piece of shit. If you hadn't pushed your girlfriend over the cliff, then we'd be heading for home now and Peter wouldn't be on a stretcher."

"You take that back," Sam shouted, his voice crackling with emotion. "I didn't do anything to Gayle."

"Yeah, you keep telling yourself that, Killer."

"Stop it, the pair of you," said Martin, like an overstressed dad who's had enough. He stopped walking abruptly and the stretcher rocked. Jo thought they were going to drop Peter for a moment.

"Nobody knows what happened for sure," he continued, "but we need to work together to get Peter to the farmhouse. Once we have, you two can have a fight or do whatever you want but for the moment, leave it alone."

Sam looked away and Jo could see his eyes were shiny with tears. Tony looked at Martin as if sizing him up. Tension crackled in the air.

"You reckon?" Tony asked quietly.

Jo had the awful sense of impending violence, like standing too close to a pair of arguing drunks in a pub. It wasn't a question of when something was going to happen, but how bad it would be.

"I do," said Martin carefully. He kept eye contact with Tony.

"You know as well as I do that it's his fault we're here, Martin," said Tony.

"You're a prick," muttered Sam.

"And you're a killer," countered Tony. "So I guess you win."

The man was impossible. "You don't know he's a killer," Jo said.

"Oh, really?" Tony asked sarcastically.

"Yes," she said. "Really." Her annoyance at his bullying pushed back any fear she might have at him lashing out. "There's four of us here and any one of us could have done it."

Tony smirked and jutted his chin towards Martin. "Is that your wife confessing?"

"Hardly," she said. "I just want to get to the farm."

"And anyway," Tony said. "What if there were five suspects?"

"You think Peter did it?" Sam asked in surprise.

"You're an idiot," Tony said. "I'm talking about that bloke I saw on the hill yesterday, the one with the bald head."

Tony looked like he was serious. Although there must be millions of bald men in the country, it chilled her that Tim might be making good on his threat that night in the car park – 'When you turn around, I'll be there'. She didn't think there was any weight to his threat, it was just something he'd said to scare her but what if she was wrong? She'd misread him before.

"All the more reason to get Peter to safety and for us to get going," said Martin. "We're wasting time."

"You stopped," Tony said.

With a sigh, Martin signalled for him to move and they started walking again. The gradient of the slope got steeper and by the time they reached the ridge they were all breathing heavily. The farmhouse was clearly visible now and looked the worse for wear.

"I can't see any phone wires," said Sam.

"Shit," said Martin.

They threaded their way around a handful of trees onto a narrow lane that led off to the left. Heavy vehicles had gouged deep tyre tracks in it and left a thick grassy strip growing in the middle. A high stone wall enclosed the farmhouse and the second-floor windows seemed to glare at them like dark eyes.

"I wonder where that lane goes?" Sam asked.

"Who cares?" said Tony.

"I do, because we're not getting over that wall," said Martin.

"There has to be a way in," Jo said, "because Peter was planning to come here." She looked down the lane. "I think there's a gate further down."

They walked along the lane with the incline in their favour now. The tyre ruts weren't level but made for a more even walk than the meadow hillside had.

The wall abruptly dropped to waist-height and Jo got a good look at the farmhouse. The roof had a big hole near the central chimney and a lot of tiles were missing. On this side a ramshackle building with a sagging roof that might have been a barn or garage was attached to the house. More barns were out the back and each looked in as much disrepair as the others.

"That looks rough," said Martin.

"Good eggs, though, apparently," said Tony.

The large lawn in front of the farmhouse was patchy and pitted. Piles of machinery were barely visible in a tangle of undergrowth. A gravel track ran across the top of the lawn towards a wooden fence on the far side that had an unruly hedge growing through it. A five-bar gate led onto the moors.

"I wonder if they have a car?" Sam asked.

"It'd help if they did," Jo said.

The five-bar double-width gate was fifty yards or so further on and secured by a chain and padlock.

A dog started barking and more joined in until it sounded like there was a pack of them.

"That's a lot of dogs," said Tony. "They don't sound happy."

"For fuck's sake," said Martin. "Can't anything go right today?"

"I could climb over," Jo said. If the guard dogs were loose, they'd have been running towards them by now.

Martin was aghast. "Are you mad?"

"No. I'll climb over and get the lady in the farm to open the gate for us."

"Let her go if she wants to," said Tony.

"Except it's not your wife climbing into a yard where dogs are barking."

"No, because she's not here. But if she was and offered, I'd let her go."

"Easy for you to say," said Sam and he didn't flinch when Tony glared at him.

"I hardly need your permission," said Jo. "And I won't be stupid. If dogs appear, I'll run back."

They lowered Peter to the ground, which seemed to wake him momentarily. He muttered "What's happening?" then grimaced and drifted off again.

Jo climbed on top of the gate and took in the field, the path and the house. She couldn't see any animals even though more dogs seemed to be barking now. She lowered herself over and brushed off her hands.

"Take it easy," said Martin.

"What's the worst thing that could happen?" she asked.

"Those dogs could get out," said Sam.

"Yeah, thanks," she said. "You're not helping."

She walked with purpose along the gravel track and watched the house, alert for movement in the two downstairs windows but saw nothing. All she could hear was the crunch of her boots on the gravel and the increasing din of the unseen dogs. Her heart thumped and tension seemed to fill her joints with lead.

Jo stopped at the front door and the slightest movement caught her eye in the window to her right. She waved then looked for a doorbell or knocker but couldn't find one. She rapped her knuckles as hard as she could on the rough surface.

A red kite called and the wind whistled mournfully for a moment as if replying.

She knocked again and, this time, heard something from inside.

"Hello?" she called. "I'm sorry to bother you, but we need your help."

She heard a tapping then a rolling sound.

"My name's Jo Harper. Our hiking guide's been hurt."

A chain rattled and a latch clicked. The door opened slowly on protesting hinges. An acrid smell hit Jo and made her flinch. The door opened wider to reveal a dark hallway and then she saw an old woman half in shadow standing behind a walking frame. It was difficult to see her face but the shotgun resting on the top of the frame was clear to see.

Chapter 27

Shock rippled through Jo and she involuntarily took a step back.

"What's up there, missus?" the old woman asked. She sounded out of breath and the shotgun barrel dipped up and down as she spoke. A puppy rushed through the old woman's legs and stood at the threshold, yapping at Jo. "Ignore that ball of fluff and answer the question." The old woman wiggled the shotgun. "We get a lot of people up here looking for ordnance and for some reason they think there's a load in here." The old woman tilted her head to one side like a curious puppy. "You don't look like you're after old bombs and bullets."

"We're not," said Jo quickly. "It's just that our guide, Peter, has badly broken his leg. We need–"

"Peter? You mean Peter Roth?"

"Yes, that's the one."

"So, why're you sneaking around like Modesty Blaise?" The old woman came forward out of the shadow. Her face was deeply lined and her eyes were dulled with age. An elastic band held her thinning hair in a top knot and her lips were pale lines. She wore a housecoat with a ripped pocket and a man's watch, which dwarfed her bony wrist. "Where's Peter, then?"

Jo risked a glance away from the shotgun. Martin had climbed over the gate and was reaching for the poles as the other two struggled to lift the stretcher. "There," she said and pointed.

The old woman edged forward with her walker and the shotgun barrel bobbed.

"I'm not going to hurt you," Jo said.

The old woman frowned. "I expect not," she said then seemed to realise she was holding a weapon. "Oh, this? It hasn't been loaded since my Charlie died some twenty years back. I keep it by the door because it gives people the willies and I like scaring the shit out of those idiot treasure hunters." Her smile revealed two teeth in her upper gum and three in her lower. "Sorry I scared you, missus. My name's Molly and this is what's left of my farm."

Relief ran through Jo like a cooling hand. "Thank you, Molly, and I understand completely."

Molly squinted as if trying to see the truth in Jo's eyes. Seemingly satisfied, she leaned the shotgun against the wall. "So, what happened to Peter?"

Jo quickly explained the morning's events and Molly listened intently.

"That sounds bad," she said. "Was the girl suicidal?"

"I have no idea, but it didn't seem like it to me."

"When did you meet her?"

"Yesterday, just before we started the hike."

"Can you vouch for any of those?" Molly asked and gestured towards the three men.

"Only the one in the blue jacket with greying hair. He's my husband."

"So do you think one of those other buggers pushed her over?" Molly asked as if it was a perfectly normal question.

"Peter told me to be careful," she said quietly.

"Sounds like he thought it, then. What can I do to help, missus?"

"Jo," she reminded her.

"I know, you already told me."

"Oh. Well I'd like to borrow your phone, to call the authorities. We need to get mountain rescue to try and get Peter down safely, and also to recover Gayle's body."

"I don't have a phone, missus."

"Not even a mobile?"

"Nope."

Jo couldn't believe someone would live out on the moor like this without a means to communicate. "How do you get in touch with people?"

"I see the postman most days and he brings messages and stuff. Then my son calls in once a week or so."

It didn't answer what Molly would do if she needed to report an emergency, and made Jo's worry grow. If they couldn't get in touch with the authorities, then what would they do with Peter?

The others had managed to get him over the gate and were now trudging along the path with Martin holding both front poles. The puppy ventured onto the gravel and barked his displeasure at the interlopers as he danced around Jo's feet.

Martin stopped behind Jo. "Hello, I'm Martin Harper. I assume my wife's told you we've had a bit of an issue. Peter's broken his leg and I think he's got concussion."

"Sounds like a lot more than a bit of an issue, I'd say," said Molly.

"Another issue is that Molly doesn't have a phone," said Jo.

"Brilliant," muttered Tony.

"Why don't you get him indoors?" Molly asked. "We can figure out what to do then."

"Good idea," said Jo.

"Hold this." Sam waited until Tony grasped the pole. Sam shook out his arms then took his phone from his pocket. "No signal here."

"That's what my son's always saying," said Molly.

"I'll see if I can get one on the higher ground beyond the gate," said Sam and walked away.

Molly turned the walking frame and made her way back into the shadows. She looked over her shoulder at Jo. "Well, missus, are you coming?"

Jo stepped into the hall and the acrid smell intensified enough she had to put her fingers against her nostrils. A staircase ran up the wall to her right and there were at least two piles of yellowing newspapers on every riser. There were several dog bowls dotted across the piles and some still held food old enough to have congealed.

The hallway was made narrower by more piles of newspapers and the occasional leaning tower of paperbacks. When Jo could see the carpet, it was threadbare and old. More puppies appeared and threaded between Molly's feet and the walking frame wheels as they barked at the intruders.

"Ignore the fluffs," Molly said and pushed opened a door to her left.

The room was compact and smelled overpoweringly of dog food and something unpleasant that might have been dog excrement or the decaying remains of something. An old leather sofa dominated the space and there were more piles of newspapers. A small table stood in front of the window.

"Help me clear those fluffs off the settee then your menfolk can put Peter on there."

It didn't seem the most hygienic option to Jo but she supposed beggars couldn't be choosers. She carefully picked up a couple of puppies and put them on the floor. One darted behind a pile of newspapers which set off a round of barking and the other climbed back onto the sofa. She picked it up again.

"Bugger," said Molly. She took a tissue out of her pocket and wiped at something on one of the cushions. "Ah well, what Peter doesn't know won't hurt him."

"No," said Jo and felt nauseous. She went back into the hall still carrying the puppy. "Bring Peter in here."

Molly came up behind her. "They'd better be careful of my paintwork."

"They will," said Jo. "I don't suppose you have a car, do you?"

"There's one in the garage."

Jo felt a quick surge of joy. "Would you mind if we borrowed it? That would really help us."

"Why would I mind?" Molly asked. "It's the first barn on the corner. Hold on a second." She dug into the pocket of her housecoat and came out with a set of keys she handed to Jo. "You'll need these."

"Thanks."

Jo put the puppy on the stairs and walked out and around the side of the house. The dogs were louder from here. The barn was next to the house and the double doors were padlocked shut. She went around the side and found an unlocked single door which opened easily.

A dark red Morris Marina, paled by dust, stood on the hard-packed mud floor. Jo wondered how long it had been since it was used and whether the battery would have any life left. She walked around the back of the car and straight into a spider's web. After a quick dance to get it all off her face and out of her hair she opened the driver's door. A single egg lay on the driver's seat. She gently moved it onto the passenger seat then sat behind the wheel.

She shifted the car into neutral and the gear change was as smooth as running a hot knife through butter. She put the key in the ignition and turned it but didn't even hear the click of a starter motor. She tried again but still nothing.

Jo felt under the steering column for the bonnet release then got out of the car and walked around to the front. She pulled open the bonnet and there was no engine or gearbox. A bird had made a massive nest in the engine space.

"Shit." She slammed the bonnet shut.

Someone walked along the gravel on the other side of the double doors and she followed their progress as they came around the side of the garage. The person paused and dogs barked.

The door opened.

Chapter 28

In mounting panic, Jo put the car between her and whoever it was.

Tony stepped cautiously into the garage and it took him a moment to see her. "Hello there," he said.

"I thought you were helping Martin with Peter." The idea of sharing this enclosed space with him scared her and she hated him for making her feel like that.

"I've already done it. I told him I wanted to get some air."

"So why are you in here with me?"

"Keep your hair on, princess." He held up his hands in a peace-keeping gesture. "I was just checking everything was fine."

"It's really not," she said. With every one of them a suspect, why would he think she'd be comfortable being alone with him?

"With you or the car?"

"The car. It hasn't got an engine."

"So why did the daft old bat let you come and check it out?"

"Who knows?"

"Looks like we're bloody walking back then." Tony checked his watch. "It's almost midday. We'd better get moving." He stepped to one side, as if waiting for her to come around the car and walk past him.

"I'll follow you out," she said.

He looked at her as though weighing up her decision then shrugged. "Fair enough, love."

She waited until he'd left the garage and then followed him outside.

"Do you think I had anything to do with what happened to Gayle?" he asked. His voice was level and his tone neutral.

"It doesn't really matter what I think, does it?" she said and he raised his eyebrows. "If it was you, you'd never tell me because you know I'd tell Martin then you'd have me and him to deal with. All I have to do now is shout and he'll be out and you'll be caught."

"So does your list of suspects include Martin or is it just me and Sam?"

"Why would I think it was Martin? He didn't know Gayle."

"Neither did I," said Tony with a sly smile. "I heard someone mooching around the tents last night and they didn't wander off into the trees for a piss."

Had he heard the same person as her? Or was he lying and that person was actually him? Her mind raced but didn't seem to be able to properly connect anything at the moment.

"It doesn't make sense to me to focus on anyone other than Sam," he said with a steely edge to his tone. "But you throw your suspicions where you want because it doesn't matter if you wrongly accuse someone, does it?"

"I haven't accused anyone," she protested.

"Not much you haven't." He turned on his heel and stalked away around the garage towards the house.

She followed him at a slower pace once he was out of the way.

* * *

137

Martin was helping to settle Peter on the sofa when Jo went into the lounge. "Hey," she said.

Peter raised his head gently and gave her a sad smile. "Hello, Jo."

She knelt beside him. "How are you feeling?"

"Like death warmed up, if you'll pardon the expression in light of this morning's events." He touched her hand. "Thank you for helping to get me up from the plateau."

"We could hardly leave you there, could we?" she asked.

"Did you check the car?" Martin asked.

"The car's not going anywhere."

Peter laughed then squeezed his eyes shut with pain and put a hand to his forehead. "You were planning to borrow Molly's car?"

"Yes," said Martin with an air of exasperation. "Nothing's going right. Sam can't get a signal, Molly hasn't got a landline and now we're going to have to carry you back."

"You don't have to," Peter said. "Leave me here. I'll be safe with Molly and my leg's not going to get any more broken sitting on this sofa. You lot are fit and healthy so it shouldn't take you long to reach the quarry, then it's all downhill to Hadley Hall."

"I think you're making it sound easier than it will be," said Martin.

"Hardly," said Peter and he pulled gently on Jo's hand. "But I think you should stay here with me."

"Why? I'm in better shape than Tony and Sam, why not leave them here?"

"Because I don't trust them," Peter said quietly enough that both Martin and Jo had to lean in. "I meant what I said this morning. Gayle didn't take a wrong turn. Someone pushed her over the cliff and it wasn't me and I'm pretty sure it wasn't Jo. Which leaves those two." He looked at Martin. "And you. No offence."

Martin rolled his eyes. "None taken."

"I think whoever it was made a mistake and got the wrong person. It was dark, she was wearing your jacket."

"I didn't meet any of them until yesterday." Jo looked searchingly at Peter and he met her gaze for a moment then glanced at Martin. She looked at her husband too and he looked sheepish at first then annoyed.

"Hey, don't get any funny ideas," he said. "I don't want to hurt you."

"I know," she said. It was a ridiculous idea. Whatever had been going on, Martin wasn't a violent man and rarely lost his temper. To suggest he would organise this holiday just to push her over a cliff would suggest psychotic levels of premeditation.

"There is the person Tony said he saw ahead of us yesterday," Martin pointed out.

"We never did catch up with him, did we?" Peter said.

"No." Martin shook his head. "It feels like there's something obvious here that we're just not seeing."

Jo bit her lip. Should she tell him her suspicion even though it made no sense?

"Well whoever it is," Peter said, "we can't leave them here because I'm in no fit shape to protect Molly."

"I'm not staying," Jo said. "If Tony or Sam did it then Martin might be in danger. There's safety in numbers."

"Sounds like you've made your mind up," said Peter. He leaned back on the sofa and closed his eyes. "My head is killing me."

"Get some rest," said Jo. "It'll do you good." She couldn't remember from her first aid courses at work if you were supposed to let concussed people sleep or not. "Though maybe you shouldn't fall asleep."

Peter murmured something but didn't open his eyes.

Sam came into the room with his lip curled and a hand against his nose.

"Did you find a signal?" Jo asked.

"Not one fucking bar. What the hell is this place? Everything looks sticky and smells. There are puppies everywhere."

"Don't worry about that," said Martin. "Did you see Tony?"

"He was in the garage with me," Jo said.

Martin's head snapped around to face her. "What do you mean?" He sounded angry, like it was her fault. "Why were you in the garage alone with him?"

"It wasn't my bloody idea, Martin. He just turned up."

"Fucking hell. He told me he was going out to get a breath of fresh air."

Molly came into the room. "I've put the kettle on. Everyone want a cup of tea?"

Sam looked around the room with obvious distaste and shook his head. Martin and Jo politely declined.

"Well, that's a shame." She glanced at Peter. "Is he dead?"

"Resting his eyes," said Jo. "We're going to head off now."

"Are you taking the car?"

"No thanks," said Jo. "We'll probably be quicker walking."

"Do you know the way?"

Martin pointed vaguely towards the back of the house. "North?" he said.

Tony came into the room. "Who's heading north?" he asked. Jo saw Martin glare at him but if Tony noticed he didn't show it.

"We are," Martin said through gritted teeth. "We're hiking back to Hadley Hall."

"Well, if that's where you're going," said Molly, "you definitely need to go north."

"Peter said something about us walking by a quarry," said Jo.

"Aye, big old quarry up that way. Make sure you take care. We've had people in the past fall over the edge of that to their deaths."

Sam looked at his feet and Jo saw his chin wobble. "We'll be careful," she said.

"Have you got a map?" Molly asked.

Tony pulled it out of his pocket. "I have it."

"Put it on the table," said Molly and she shooed some puppies off it. Sam picked one up and put it on the floor. It cocked its leg against the sofa then ran off to join its siblings.

Tony spread the map out. "Do we have to walk across the meadow, or can we use that track beside your house?"

"Hardly," Molly said. "Didn't you come up on it?"

"We didn't find it until we'd come through the trees," said Jo.

Molly laughed. "Are you telling me you carried that stretcher across the meadow?" She laughed again. "My goodness, that must have taken you bloody ages."

"It did," said Martin. "Was there a shortcut?" He glared again at Tony who shrugged.

"Of course. That track starts just behind the trees on the plateau and runs right up to my house. That's how my son's able to drive down and put the supplies in the little brick store."

"For fuck's sake," said Sam. "I thought you said you could read a map."

Tony rounded on him. "Zip it, Killer. I didn't hear you offer to read the map."

"Enough," said Martin.

Sam looked like he was about to say something but then thought better of it.

"I'm sorry, Molly," continued Martin. "Can you show us where we need to go?"

"Aye." Molly took a pair of half-moon glasses from the pocket of her smock. She peered intently at the map then pointed at the quarry. "That's where you're heading." She traced a finger back and then prodded the map. "That's where we are. So just go from here to there and you're sorted."

"How far would you say it was?" asked Martin.

"Dunno, never walked it. But probably six or seven miles. Most of it uphill though."

"Typical," said Tony.

He gathered the map up and Martin checked Peter was comfortable.

Jo touched Molly's arm. "Thanks," she said. "You've been wonderful. We'll get someone to help Peter as soon as we can."

"I trust you, missus. You take care yourself. I listened to what Peter said about your friend who went over." Molly held her hand for a moment. "I have something for you. Peter said you lost your coat." Molly reached behind the door and pulled out a red and black Regatta fleece. "Take this. It's my granddaughter's but you're about the same size and she doesn't need it right now."

"Thank you," said Jo and pulled the fleece on. It smelled vaguely of dogs but fitted just right. "I appreciate it."

"When that wind blows at the top of the valley you feel it right in your bones," said Molly. "Now, I'd better go and sort Peter's tea out. You four take care of yourselves, you hear?"

Chapter 29

"Weird old bat," said Tony.

"She can read a map better than you, though," Sam said.

As if he'd been waiting for the jibe, Tony planted both hands on Sam's chest and pushed him against the wall.

"Keep going, Killer," he said and leaned in close. "You might have scared your girlfriend, but you don't scare me."

The sudden violence startled Jo. Martin grabbed Tony's shoulder. Tony tried to shrug him off, but Martin pulled him away. Sam looked shell-shocked.

"That's enough," Martin said.

Jo's surprise shifted to anger at the machismo. "You've got fifty pounds on him, Tony, just leave him alone. The pair of you need to stop showing off."

"I wasn't showing off," muttered Sam.

"You've been on at each other all morning," she said and glared at him. "It's like you're trying to see who can pee up a wall the highest."

"So let's leave him here then," said Tony as he shrugged off Martin's hand. "You don't need to hold on to me. The lanky fucker's not worth it."

"We can't leave him here because then Peter and Molly wouldn't be safe," said Martin. He drew a rough circle in the air that encompassed all of them. "One of us pushed Gayle off the cliff, in case you'd forgotten."

"I didn't forget," said Sam quietly.

"And it's weird that you're not in floods of tears at the idea of losing your girlfriend," said Tony.

"That's not fair," Jo said. "People cope with trauma differently."

"So now you're sticking up for him?" Tony demanded. "You didn't jump to my defence."

"You hardly need my help," she said.

"But Killer does, does he?"

Sam moved but Martin stepped between the two men. "Pack it in, the pair of you. It could be any of us. We can't trust anyone."

"You don't trust Jo?" Tony asked.

"Oh, fuck off," Martin said.

"I didn't hurt Gayle," Sam protested. "I was in a tent with you all night, Martin. You'd have heard me move."

"So did you hear him move?" Tony asked.

"I don't know," said Martin.

"Same question to you, Killer. Did Martin move at all?"

"No," said Martin and Sam shook his head.

"Maybe you're both lying because you threw the bimbo off the cliff together."

"She wasn't a bimbo," said Jo.

Tony looked at her with surprise. "Who gives a fuck? As I see it, we have two suspects, your husband and Lanky lad. So why don't you and me stay here while those two go off."

"I don't want to stay here with you," Jo said. "And you were in a tent of your own with nobody to hear you, so you're a prime suspect too."

Tony threw up his arms. "For fuck's sake." He jabbed a finger at Sam. "I'm telling you it's him."

"That's your story," said Martin, "but it could be any of us. Between here and the hotel we keep together and watch each other's backs. How does that sound? The only time we separate is for a piss break."

"That makes sense," said Tony. He patted Martin on the shoulder. "And thanks for pulling me away from Killer here, he could have pushed me into doing something I'd have regretted."

"Don't worry about it," said Martin. "We're all hyped up." He raised his eyebrows in query at Jo. "Are you okay?"

The whole exchange had tired her out and she was fed up with it. "Yes, I just want to get back now."

* * *

They retraced their steps up the lane to a dry-stone wall that was slowly being reclaimed by nature.

The view from the top of it was glorious and Jo would probably have taken a moment or two to appreciate it under different circumstances.

The meadow they were about to cross rose at a steady incline to a ridge where trees poked towards the sky like spines. It was at least three or four miles away and looked like tough going. There was a lot of scrubland and several outcrops of rock the size of cars.

"There he is," said Tony and pointed towards the far ridge. "He's up near the trees."

Jo's stomach dropped. She squinted into the distance but couldn't see any movement.

"I can't see anyone," said Sam. He was looking at the display on the back of his GoPro.

"That's still MoD land," said Martin. He shielded his eyes with his hand. "You heard what Peter said."

"If it's the same bloke I saw yesterday, then he clearly doesn't give a shit. Maybe he hurt Gayle? I mean, it makes as much sense as one of you three murdering her does."

"But where has he been?" asked Martin. "How did he get so far ahead without us seeing him on the meadow?"

"They didn't spend ages dragging some old crock to a farmhouse, did they?"

"No," said Martin and looked towards the trees with curiosity. "I can't see anyone."

"I didn't imagine it and I'm sure it was the same bloke. He had a bald head and beard."

Jo felt like she'd stepped into a cold shower.

"How did you see a beard from this distance?" Sam asked.

"Well, he either had a beard or a scarf over his mouth."

'Shit,' Jo thought. 'Could it really be Tim?'

"Are we heading for those trees?" Martin asked.

Tony took out the map. "No, we'd be better off following that line," he said and pointed towards a trail other hikers had walked into the grass. "That'll take us over the ridge to the left and we can come down onto the quarry side there."

"Keeping us away from that bloke sounds good to me," said Martin. "There's no point inviting problems when we already have enough of the bastards. We should get going."

Jo kept watch on the trees but still couldn't see anything.

The group moved without her and spread out as they went, with Sam taking the higher ground as he held up his phone for a signal. Tony took the middle path while Martin was to the right. After a few paces he turned.

"You coming?" he called to her.

"Yes," she said and jogged to catch up with him. "Did you see that person in the trees?"

"At that distance I wouldn't be able to make out someone if they were wearing neon and waving. Did you see them?"

"No," she said and shook her head. "But I have something to tell you."

Chapter 30

Martin, Three Weeks Ago

Martin winced as each blow landed with a sickening thud.

Rick Browne was struggling. The last right hook had opened up his eyebrow and the spray of blood painted a line upon the coat of a woman standing ringside. She'd brayed with delight as she showed off her memento to her partner.

Kilburn Farm was on the eastern edge of Hadlington and Martin could smell the cattle as soon as they had turned off the main road. The farm was at the end of a long drive and they had passed the main house and a couple of smaller barns before a teenager directed them onto a large concrete apron in front of a larger one.

"Mind the cow shit," Gordy said as he got out. "I don't want any in my new car."

"That's not going to be easy," Martin said. Cowpats of varying colour and consistency covered the ground. There were some very impressive vehicles parked against the building and the owners, all young men with slicked-back hair wearing a lot of gold jewellery, leaned on the cars and looked cool. Young women in revealing dresses moved between each car in small groups.

"What is this?" Martin asked as they joined a steady stream of punters making their way from the car park.

"A big deal," said Gordy.

Martin had four thousand pounds in twenties and he tapped his inside pocket to check the envelope was there. It was. He walked with one hand on it.

"You don't need to do that," said Gordy. "Nobody's going to touch it."

"It's a lot of money."

"Take a look at these cars, boss. Your stash is small change to these geezers."

The tournament was in the barn furthest from the house. People milled at the open doors and from inside Martin could hear music, conversation and laughter. As they got closer, his nerves increased.

"This is a bad idea, Gordy."

"So you keep saying, but I haven't heard a better suggestion yet."

Fluorescent strip lights had been fitted to the exposed joists inside the barn and people sat on hay bales all around the sides. A ring had been set up in the middle, but the posts weren't padded and neither was the ground. A man sat on a deck chair off to one side behind a picnic table with a big bell on it. A large crowd surrounded the ring.

Three burly men were in the ring helping the loser of the last bout to his feet while the victor was led away by his corner man. The loser had so much blood on his face that his teeth almost glowed.

"That's where we lay the bets," said Gordy and pointed to four tables at the back end of the barn. "We'll meet back here when we're done."

"Got you," said Martin and willed his nerves down as he walked around the ring. He saw the odds boards and understood them, and that, for a moment, made him feel a little more in control. Bookies in sharp suits shouted further odds as they handled large wads of cash and gave out tickets. The air was thick with tension and excitement and Martin could feel both emotions keenly. This thrill was the only thing he'd found hard to give up all those years ago when Jo bailed him out.

He took his time checking the odds and decided it would make sense to put fifteen hundred on two of them and a grand on the third.

Once he'd collected all three slips, he put them into the envelope and stashed that in his pocket. Gordy was waiting by the time he got back to the ring.

They watched two fights before Rick's was due to start. Both were quick and brutal, the gloves were barely padded judging by the amount of damage the fighters quickly inflicted on one another. Martin had never been a big fan of boxing and he'd certainly never seen so much blood spilled. Both losers had to be carried out of the ring and the second looked to be unconscious.

"Brutal," said Gordy.

"You're telling me."

A man in his early thirties, wearing a Stone Island jacket and black jeans, was doing the announcing and he climbed into the ring now and put his megaphone to his mouth.

"Next on the bill is Rick Browne against Joey 'The Pepper' Wynn. No more bets on this fight."

The announcer got out of the ring as the boxers came through the main doors and made their way through the crowd flanked by their corner men.

"That's our boy," said Gordy pointing towards a tall, muscular man who looked like he was barely into his twenties. He had close-cropped blonde hair and a tattoo of a green man on his right shoulder. One of his corner men, with cauliflower ears and a misshapen nose, raised his hand and Gordy returned the gesture. "And that's Hughie."

The other fighter must have been at least ten years older and perhaps half a stone heavier if not more. He was bald and his pate gleamed in the light. He was running to seed, more bulky than muscular, and both of his arms were sleeved in a variety of colours and images.

The fighters got into the ring and circled one another. The crowd moved closer to the ropes. Martin watched Rick shake out his hands and look towards Hughie. Hughie nodded and stuck up his thumb.

The bell sounded and the crowd went quiet for a moment then someone shouted for Rick and a woman screamed with excitement. The boxers continued to circle. Rick held out his right hand and Joey slapped it away.

"Come on," someone shouted. "Fucking hit him."

Joey dropped his shoulder and went in low. Rick tried to counter it but Joey wasn't playing fair and his first punch caught Rick square in the groin. Rick bent over as he staggered back and Joey went with him. He landed three good punches to the ribs and an upper cut that sent the younger fighter into the corner.

"Fuck," said Gordy.

Joey went in hard and Rick tried to hit back but couldn't get the leverage and ended up grabbing his opponent to stop him from hitting. People in the crowd booed.

Rick wiped blood from his eyes and followed Joey as he backed away. They circled for a moment then Rick made a move. Joey struggled against the punches and, very soon, it was obvious the older man's stamina wasn't a match for his opponent.

After letting himself get punched back into the ropes, Joey came back and hit Rick in the ribs with a quick combination. He focussed on the right-hand side which caused the younger man to twist himself out of the way.

Martin's heart raced. His mouth was dry and he felt sick. He didn't know a lot about boxing, but it didn't take an expert to know something was very wrong here. If Rick was going to produce some kind of comeback, then he was going to have to do it quickly.

Joey kneed Ricky in the groin and the crowd hollered their delight.

"Hey!" shouted Gordy.

A man in front turned around with a sneer. "What's your problem, snowflake?"

"He's kneeing him in the bollocks."

"So what? The lad can knee him back."

The man went back to watching the match and Martin leaned in close to Gordy. "You said he was a shoo-in. What's going on?"

"No idea."

Martin watched Hughie shout advice. Rick moved around the ring warily, his defence dropping as he tried to protect his face and groin at the same time. Joey shook out his arms and bared his mouth guard then feinted towards Rick. The younger boxer stepped back quickly and the crowd yelled at him. Some people were laughing. Rick was clearly out of his element.

"He's going to get killed," said Martin.

"So are we," said Gordy.

Joey feinted left but went right and caught Rick on the temple with a glancing blow. Rick staggered, clearly dazed and Joey drove him back into the corner with jabs and wild swings.

"No!" shouted Gordy. "Get out of there."

Joey pressed his advantage with vicious blows to Rick's ribs and head before he kneed him again. Rick was barely conscious and the cut over his eye bled freely now. He slid down the post. Martin heard each punch over the din of the crowd.

Hughie ran around the ring and threw a towel directly at Joey. It didn't make any difference as Joey punched Rick onto the ground. Hughie climbed through the ropes and Joey's man followed him in to break the fight up. Joey struggled to keep going and then seemed to snap out of his rage and paraded around the ring with his arms over his head. Blood was speckled across his chest and face.

Gordy pushed forward and Martin followed in his wake. They held the ropes apart so Hughie could get Rick through. The boxer was unsteady on his feet and his eyes were unfocussed.

"What the fuck happened, Hughie?"

Hughie propped Rick against the post and wiped his cut eye with a cloth. "Joey Pepper's a fucking ringer, that's what happened. He's a big bloke and out of shape but he's got a punch like a mule's kick. The poor kid didn't stand a chance." He looked at Gordy. "Did you lay on any bets?"

"Every last fucking penny, Hughie," Gordy said. "Every last fucking penny."

Chapter 31

"And that's the whole story," Jo said.

Martin hadn't interrupted while she told him about the incident in Ratty's but his face had clouded with anger. "Why didn't you tell me about him before?"

She'd asked herself the same question a lot. It wasn't as if she'd led Tim on or given him any cause to think there might be a connection between them. "I don't know," she said. "I wish I had, though, because now it feels like this is a confession told out of guilt."

"There's no confession to make, sweetheart. From what you said, he jumped to conclusions."

The comment saddened her. "I'm sorry, Martin." She reached for his hand and he took it, which warmed her. "I always said I'd tell you everything and I always have except for this and now that might be the worst decision ever, especially if it's him up in those trees."

"Well, if it is, I'll give him a good hiding for scaring you, okay? How could the fucker put you through that?"

"What if he did kill Gayle, though?" She still didn't think it likely, but it wasn't impossible. He'd lashed out in anger and maybe that had festered in him so when he saw her yesterday in that distinctive bloody jacket, he'd decided to make his move.

"Then we'll all give him a good hiding, but I'm sure it wasn't him. Maybe Tony did see someone and maybe he didn't, but from what you said, Tim sounds like a weak man preying on a woman. He probably went straight home and locked himself away for a few days."

"Do you think so?" It would give her so much reassurance if Martin agreed.

"Of course. Bullies are only tough until someone stands up to them. You know that."

"Thank you for being so understanding, Martin."

"Hey, you've been understanding of me and my work troubles." He exhaled loudly. "They didn't even make sense to me, so I had no idea how to tell you I'd got caught up in something that went wrong so quickly."

"Did someone get hurt?"

"No." He flashed a quick, tight smile. "Someone I trusted let me down and I had to carry the blame."

"What happened?"

"It's hardly worth going into detail because it's sorted now. But it made me realise I hadn't been there for you or for us."

A shout startled them both and Jo looked across the meadow to see that Tony was now standing very close to Sam. They were perhaps two or three hundred yards from the top of the ridge.

"Shit," muttered Martin. "What now?"

They broke into a cautious run and Jo kept an eye on the ground for treacherous hollows.

"What's going on?" Martin called.

"He's still fucking filming me," yelled Tony.

Sam backed away and held the GoPro to his chest like a crucifix warding off evil. "I'm not filming you, I'm filming the area. You just happened to walk in front of it."

"Jesus, Sam, can you not give it a rest?" asked Martin.

"Why should I? He's been on at me all day, you both know that. I'm the one stuck here with whoever murdered my lovely friend so why shouldn't I film everything that happens?"

His criticism was well placed and stung. Jo felt a wave of sadness from him and it seemed like the grief was eating him up. "I'm sorry I said that, Sam. But filming Tony won't help unless you're expecting him to confess."

"Hardly." Sam's eyes shone with unshed tears. "But when we get back, I can show all this footage to the police and they might be able to do something with it." A tear broke ran down his cheek and he swiped it away.

"Or you might be able to do something with it," said Tony. "You're a fucking vampire, mate. Don't film me anymore. I don't give you permission." He turned and stalked away.

Martin watched him go then slowly turned to Sam. "You're not really going to use all this in your documentary, are you?"

"What else can I do?" Sam asked.

Martin looked away in disgust.

"Come on," Jo said to Martin and they walked back to the track together.

"Is it just me or was that tragically heartless?" Martin asked when they were out of earshot. He looked at her. "Do you think he did it?"

"It doesn't feel like he would, but he might not have liked the fact Gayle wasn't into him like he was to her."

"She wasn't?"

"Not from what she told me. But what about Tony? He was leering over Gayle so maybe he pushed his luck and approached her at night and got rebuffed."

"That'd be fairly obvious though, wouldn't it? Even if he wasn't thinking right."

"Well," she said, "that only leaves the option that Peter was right and whoever did it thought she was me because of the jacket."

"But that leaves me as the prime suspect, like we said before."

"You didn't know Gayle before yesterday, though, did you?"

"Of course not, Jo. I'll be honest, I was glad when she latched onto you because she seemed a bit of a bubblehead and I didn't want to have to make conversation about bloody *Love Island* all day."

"She wasn't a bubblehead."

"And I didn't know or hurt her. I mean, you shared a tent with her so, hypothetically, if anyone could easily have sneaked out and thrown her over, it was you." He didn't say it viciously.

"You're right. Except I didn't."

"And all this time we're assuming Peter wasn't responsible."

"True. Have you asked Tony? I saw you getting pally with him."

"How would I ask him if he meant to murder Gayle or whether he was intending to do away with my wife, who he'd never met before?" He shook his head. "I'm not pally with him, either."

"Well, you've been very chatty."

"Why wouldn't I be? He works on the sites so we have a common background. I have conversations every day with people I've never seen before and will never see again."

"Do you like him?"

"He's a bit rough around the edges, but he seems alright."

"Do you really think so?"

"I wouldn't have said it otherwise, would I? I know you weren't a fan from the start."

"I'm not. He enjoys pushing everyone's buttons and he was really creepy with Gayle."

"Just because you don't like someone, doesn't mean they're guilty."

"True, but it doesn't mean they're not guilty either."

Tony was now on the ridge and raised his hand when Jo looked at him. She waved back.

"I just wish we were at the hotel with the police and getting everything sorted," she said.

"It won't be long now," Martin said to her, then shouted to Tony, "Keep your eyes peeled for your man in the trees. We might have to deal with him later."

Chapter 32

Martin, One Week Ago

Martin was in the warehouse loading the van when he heard someone come in. He didn't turn around because there were always people about.

Powerful hands grabbed his shoulders, lifted him to his feet and threw him against the van door. He bounced off it but kept to his feet. Sandy regarded him like a lump of dog mess he'd accidentally stepped in.

"Morning, Martin." He wore a dark suit and took a pair of brown leather gloves out of his pocket that he slowly put on.

"Hi, Sandy. How're you?"

"Can't complain." Sandy flexed his fingers once the gloves were on then looked at Martin. "Which means I'm neither happy or unhappy."

"Okay."

"Is there anything you want to tell me?"

"No." He still had a fortnight on the loan and nobody else knew about the stupidity at Kilburn Farm so he was safe.

"Oh." Sandy pouted and quickly jabbed Martin in the belly with a flat hand.

The pain was intense and Martin fell back against the door as he struggled to breathe. "What was that for?"

Sandy moved in close and grabbed Martin's left ear and twisted down. With a guttural sound, Martin was forced to squat in front of the enforcer.

"My first impression was that you were stupid since you followed Gordy into the office and asked for a loan. But I checked you out and you're supposed to be a smart bloke, even if you did slug Murray Norris. Then I heard how you got cleaned out at the farm and realized my first impression was accurate."

Sandy raised his eyebrows as if waiting for Martin to speak but Martin couldn't think of anything to say that wouldn't confirm Sandy's opinion of him.

"Were you betting to try and make back your capital for Mr McLain?"

"Yes." There was clearly no sense in denying it. "I thought it would work."

"You really are stupid, aren't you?" Sandy chuckled. "Did you think you could go to a tournament like that and spread your bet and nobody would notice?"

"I was told Rick Browne was a good fighter."

"Oh aye." Sandy let go of Martin's ear and took a step back. "He is but he's a straight arrow and like a lot of times in this life, being a straight arrow doesn't get you anywhere." He cleared his throat. "Which leads me neatly to the business I wanted to talk to you about this morning."

Martin rubbed his ear and got slowly to his feet. "Gordy showed me what you did to his finger."

"That little love tap? It didn't really cause him any serious damage, but it did help focus his mind. That's one of the things I do for Mr McLain, you see. I focus attention."

Sandy's steady tone scared Martin more than what he was saying. Martin had never been in such close proximity to a man who didn't seem to care about any pain he inflicted. "I honestly don't need my attention focussed, Sandy. I know I was stupid and I'm going to get it sorted."

"I like your attitude, Martin, but it wouldn't hurt to give you a hand."

"If you break my finger then I might not be able to drive."

Sandy laughed like he'd heard a great joke. "Like I give a shit? Anyway, I'm not going to break your finger. I think you've got the wrong idea of me. The only reason I broke Gordy's finger is because he's on his own."

Martin understood immediately and the realization took his breath away.

"Ah, maybe I did underestimate you because you're a step ahead of me here, aren't you? I'd enjoy hurting you but it's much easier to focus attention by hurting someone you love. Like your wife, for example. Jo works here in town and drives a cherry-red Ford Fiesta and goes to the over-forties swimming club."

Martin's stomach felt like it had fallen to his feet.

"But in your case, I think Olivia would be the better bet."

"Olivia?" Martin retched. "You can't do that."

"I can and probably will. She's very pretty, Martin, and she's also very good at dancing, isn't she?"

"Please, Sandy…"

"The Lexington Club has a student night on Mondays and she owns that dancefloor with her lovely moves," Sandy said with a queasy mixture of appreciation and

157

sleaze. "She's going to find it hard to shake her arse with multiple leg fractures."

Tears stung Martin's eyes. "You can't do that, I'll…"

"You'll what? Pay back the money you borrowed? Yes, you will. But if you miss the deadline, we move you onto a payment plan and sweet, pretty Olivia will be in a cast for weeks."

"Please don't hurt her," Martin begged. "She's only a teenager. None of this is anything to do with her."

Sandy punched Martin in the belly. The blow folded him over and he dropped to his knees, winded.

"All actions have consequences, Martin. I thought you'd have known that."

Chapter 33

The view from the ridge was spectacular but Jo barely noticed. All four of them were out of breath and the incline had taken more out of Jo's calves and thighs than she'd expected.

Tony led the way along the ridge path which was wide and relatively flat. The trees where Tony had seen the mystery person were a few hundred yards away and she kept watching but if someone was hiding in there, he was keeping himself well out of sight.

"I'm hungry," said Sam.

Jo looked at her watch and was surprised to see it was after two. Her stomach had been rumbling for a while.

"I pinched some protein bars out of Peter's rucksack before we left the plateau," said Martin.

"Thank God you got what you did," said Jo. Her mind had been on other things at the time. "It never occurred to me to pick up any food."

"Nor me," said Sam.

Tony had gone on ahead slightly and Martin called him. If Tony heard, he didn't show any sign and kept walking. "Hey!" Martin called again. "Let's have a break, Tony."

"I think we're near the quarry," Tony called over his shoulder. "Judging by this map, it's not too far."

Jo felt a quick surge of hope at being so near to the end.

"We need to eat something before we get there," said Martin.

"Do you think that's wise?" she asked, more sharply than she'd intended. Sam noticed because he turned the camera towards her.

"Why not?" Martin asked. "I don't fancy trying to get through a quarry on an empty stomach."

"And if I don't eat something soon," said Sam, "I'm going to pass out."

Jo couldn't tell if he was joking or not and felt an unpleasant sense of paranoia. Was he already planning on how he could bump them off before they got to safety?

"Tony!" Martin called. "We'll have a break in a minute."

"Okay but there's something up ahead by the edge of the trees. It looks like some kind of hut."

"That's where we'll stop, then," Martin said.

He didn't look overly concerned and it made Jo wonder if she was overthinking the situation. Was she being paranoid? That might explain why he wasn't thinking along the same lines as her. He was intelligent and his job relied on him being able to read people and situations so if he didn't see trouble brewing then perhaps there wasn't any.

Unless he knew who'd killed Gayle and didn't have anything to fear from them.

She shook her head to dislodge the wild accusation as quickly as possible. Martin wasn't a killer. He'd once refused to kill a half-dead pigeon a cat had savaged in their garden, so it was unlikely he'd be able to push someone over a cliff or stand by and watch someone else do it.

It would also mean that she'd been very wrong about the man she'd spent ten years of her life with and that absolutely wasn't possible. No, this was the kind of ridiculous worry that lodges in your brain at three in the morning when you can't sleep but is instantly broken into a million pieces by sunrise.

They followed the trail in silence for another few hundred yards until they reached the small brick building Tony had seen. Little more than a hut, it had a corrugated metal roof and looked like it had been there for a long time. A bare window on this side looked out over the valley and, through it, she could see another glassless window on the other side which showed a lot of trees. The door was missing and the redundant hinges were red with rust.

"What was this place?" asked Sam. He angled the camera as he moved in closer. "It looks ancient."

"Probably something to do with the quarry," said Martin. Jo stood next to him.

Tony leaned around the corner. "There're paths leading further into the trees," he reported, then walked out of sight.

"Be careful," said Martin. "If this is something to do with the quarry there might be gullies."

"What are gullies?" asked Sam as he filmed through the doorway. "Are they like bugs or animals?"

"No, they're like mini ravines. The quarry operations would use them as beds for light railways."

Tony's voice drifted to them. "Jesus. These are really steep."

Sam rushed around the building and Martin took Jo's hand and stepped off the trail. They walked through the rough grass and around the hut onto a narrow path that was being reclaimed by the undergrowth. Thin trees stood tall and the tops of them moved gently in the breeze.

Tony was on the other side of the path and they stood next to him. Jo looked down into the gully. The sides were limestone and sheer, and roots and saplings poked through gaps in the rock. The ground was perhaps ten feet down and carpeted with a mixture of rocks, branches and mulch.

"I wouldn't want to fall in," she said.

The others murmured their agreement.

"Have you got the map, Tony?" Martin asked. Tony handed it to him and Martin unfolded it. He ran his finger lightly across the paper. "There we are," he said. "And there's the quarry."

Tony leaned in to look closer. "Yeah, that's right."

"If we keep on this path then we're no more than half a mile away." He clapped Tony on the shoulder. "You picked a good route."

Jo was tempted to remind him Molly had given them the direction to head in but decided against it. "So, what now?"

"Let's eat," said Sam.

"Sounds good to me," said Tony. "But I really need a slash."

"Same here," said Sam.

"I think we could all do with going," Martin said.

"Well let's stick to the plan you suggested before," said Jo. "We don't want anyone being shoved into a gully, do we?"

"Good point," said Martin. He turned in a slow circle. "Tony, you go over towards the hut and Sam can keep on the path back towards the ridge. Me and Jo will follow this path a little way down then everyone meet back at the hut."

"Fair enough," said Tony with a smirk. "Just make sure she doesn't kill you when you turn your back."

"You're not funny," Jo said.

"Others would disagree," he said and walked away.

Sam filmed him for a moment then followed at a distance before branching off in his own direction.

* * *

"I'm so pleased we're not on camera anymore," Martin said.

"I'm getting a bit tired of it," Jo admitted.

She followed Martin. The trees were now crowded together and the space around them seemed darker and more forbidding. In the few places where the sun penetrated the canopy, the glare was piercing. Jo shielded her eyes and glanced into the gully to her right. It seemed to get deeper the further they went.

Fifty yards or so along they passed a rusted sign which read 'Quarry – Danger: Steep Cliff'. It had been used for airgun target practice and was peppered with small dents. Just beyond it was a small area on the left where someone had cleared the undergrowth and built a makeshift fire. Three large trees stood guard over it.

"How about I go in there?" Martin asked.

"Aren't we going together?"

"I don't mind, but it'd make sense for you to go further down so if one of the others does decide to make a move, they'll have to go past me first. I'll wait and stand guard for you here until you get back."

So he hadn't missed the idea of them being so close to home that the killer would make a move. "Good thinking. Just be careful, okay?"

"I'm always careful," he said. "You know me."

Jo checked neither Tony nor Sam were coming along the path then struck out away from the clearing. The trees got thicker and there were more of them and, a few feet in, the shadows were almost impenetrable. If someone were in there, she wouldn't be able to see them and the idea of that was unnerving. When she heard a bird take flight, her mind conjured up images of Tony or Sam creeping along as they followed her.

"No," she said quietly. She might not be able to shut down her paranoia, but she could stop creating scary thoughts that weren't of any help at all. She checked over her shoulder once more to make sure no one was sneaking up on her then nipped behind a tree just beyond the undergrowth. She pulled down her trousers and knickers and squatted with her back to the trunk to relieve herself.

After she'd finished, Jo started back. She kept expecting to see Martin, but the path seemed clear right the way up to the hut.

A sense of unease flickered through her as she got closer to the clearing. Had he heard something and was hiding? Had someone hurt him?

Her unease slid into panic and she ran to the clearing. Martin wasn't there. He wouldn't hide from her and had probably finished peeing before she found her spot so where was he? Had someone hit him with one of the many rocks and stones lying around? She held her breath and listened intently but couldn't hear anything untoward. She crossed the clearing and peered around the tree. He wasn't there though she could see the dampness where he'd relieved himself.

She walked back to the path. Her heartbeat was fast and loud and seemed to vibrate through her chest and into the base of her throat. She leaned forward to look over the edge of the gully just in case he'd fallen, or been pushed in. From this angle she couldn't see the ground so she stepped closer. Still not enough. She put one foot on a large rock that edged the gully.

Something cracked off to her right and startled her, sending electrical charges racing up and down her arms. Her scalp pulled tight as she looked left and right.

The path was still clear.

"Martin?" she said. Her voice sounded reedy. "Martin?" she said loudly.

If he was anywhere close, he didn't respond.

"Is there anyone there?"

There was a loud snap from behind her as if someone had stepped on a particularly dry twig. She whisked around and shielded her eyes against the sun but couldn't see anyone. Were they behind the big tree? She wasn't going to check and edged to her left, keeping her back to the gully on the assumption nobody could get to her from that direction. Two more cracks sounded in the depths of the trees.

Adrenaline pumped through her. She felt sick and more frightened than she could remember being in a long time. She quickly checked in the gully again but saw no sign of Martin. After making sure no one was coming along the path behind her, she turned and walked briskly towards the hut. The cracking noises moved with her as if someone in the trees was keeping pace. It might have been an animal or it might not. She wished Martin were here.

The sounds stopped and she slowed down to look into the trees. She still couldn't see anything in the shadowy depths.

"Martin?" She could taste bile.

Something came quickly through the trees with a lot of noise. The sun was behind them so they were little more than a silhouette. The person held something that might have been a bar or a stick and raised their arms before swinging it at her.

Jo felt the impact on her side and it punched the air from her lungs. She stumbled forward as the person swung again. This time the weapon connected with the side of her face. Brilliant points of white light burst across her field of vision even as the edges of it darkened with fluttering black drapes.

She staggered back. The person swung again and then she stepped on nothing. As the branch missed her face by inches she fell back into the gully.

Chapter 34

Jo opened her eyes slowly. Her head ached and her nose felt blocked and something was digging into her stomach.

She'd fallen into the gully but seemed to be hanging a couple of feet above the ground. The rock wall was close enough for her to touch so she grabbed for a small outcropping. Something creaked behind her and she felt a tug around her waist which pressed against the injury on her side where the man had hit her.

The image of him filled her mind's eye suddenly and, with a flash of panic, she twisted around trying to see where he was. The creaking noise came again. There was no one else in the gully, which reassured her for a moment until something snapped and she jolted slightly. She looked over her shoulder and saw her jacket had snagged on one of the root systems coming through the rocks. She reached for it, but the movement proved too much. Material tore, the wood cracked, and she was jolted again as she dropped an inch or two. She heard another much louder rip.

"Shit." The fabric of her jacket gave way and she put out her hands to try and break her fall.

The mulch cushioned her impact and she rolled onto her side, staring at the narrow strip of sky she could see above the gully. The root cluster that had caught her sprouted between two layers of the limestone rock and was snapped cleanly off. Part of her coat was still hooked on one broken end.

Jo touched her side and it was tender. She'd never known anyone break a rib in real life but was sure she'd read once that it made breathing painful, and it wasn't. She touched her face and felt wetness. There was blood on her fingertips. That frightened her and she touched the area again, gently exploring just above her jaw. The skin burned as her fingers touched a long laceration. Whatever he'd hit her with had clearly cut her and she only hoped it wasn't too deep.

The man had clearly tried to kill her and would have succeeded if she hadn't fallen into the gully. That last swing for her face could well have taken her head off had it connected.

If he'd been trying to kill her then why hadn't he checked she was dead? If he'd looked over the edge he would have seen her hanging off the side and surely would come down to finish her off.

She scrambled herself around to make sure he wasn't coming. How long had she been out of it? Did she black out temporarily or had she been unconscious for minutes? It might have taken the killer a while to find a route down into the lowest part of the gully but she had to assume he was coming and very soon. The longer she lay doing nothing, the more at risk she was.

Then she heard him.

Her throat tightened and she scrambled to her feet. The gully ran ahead in a near-enough straight line so even if she ran as fast as she could he would more than likely see her. And if she did make it to the end there was no guarantee she'd be able to climb out and that would leave her at his mercy. Panic set in and her heart and mind raced. She looked up at the wall and tried to decide if she could climb up using any hand- or footholds on the uneven rocks.

It wouldn't work.

She forced herself to breathe steadily and calm herself enough so that she could think clearly. If she didn't, this was over.

Jo looked ahead again, trying to take in everything she could see. That's when she spotted a small overhang of rock a few feet away. It was only a slight ingress, but she might be able to tuck herself under it and the minimal cover might be all she needed to go unnoticed. If the killer went by, she could work her way back in the direction he'd come. Since he would have found some way to get down there, she could use the same route to get out.

She rushed over to the ingress and crawled under the overhang. The dank earth stuck to her fingers and the sour smell of it filled her nostrils. She pushed back as far as she could, but it wasn't far enough. She shifted around and pressed herself against the rock and pulled her knees to her chest. Her fingers closed around a small stone and she picked it up. It wasn't much of a weapon, but it was better than nothing.

The man was close enough now that she could hear him breathing. He walked steadily and she supposed it was because he wasn't in a rush. He knew she was here and trapped and probably injured.

He came closer. Jo held her breath and clutched the stone. Blood rushed in her ears and pins and needles filled her fingertips.

Movement caught her eye and she pushed herself back as far as she could. The man came into view and she recognised his bright red trousers immediately, even as the overhang hid his face from her.

Chapter 35

Sam stopped in front of where she was hiding.

Jo wondered if he could see her legs. If not, then the longer he stood there, the more likely it became. Her chest burned and she let her breath out slowly between her teeth, hoping he wouldn't hear her.

Was he playing with her and getting a thrill from her fear? The idea of it made her feel sick and angry and she wanted to hurt him. If she moved quickly, she might get out from under the overhang before he had a chance to properly react. She could then throw the stone at him and even if it missed, the distraction might give her a chance to run.

"Jo?" He didn't say it very loudly and it was more of a query than anything else. It wasn't what she'd been expecting. "I can see your feet. Are you okay?"

She didn't move. He might think she was cowed and didn't want to give him that pleasure.

"Jo, I know what happened."

'Of course you do,' she thought. 'You fucking did it.'

"Are you hurt badly or can you move?"

Was he that sadistic? She'd rather he just reached in and pulled her out into the gully than play this game. She gripped the stone tightly and slid out as quickly as she could. He was too far away for her to reach easily.

Sam looked at her from behind his camera with a startled expression.

She raised the stone then saw he didn't have anything else in his hands. It didn't matter. She swung her arm and put her weight behind it but he ducked at the last moment and the stone glanced off his shoulder. He stumbled across the gully into the opposite wall and held out his free hand.

"Jo! It wasn't me, I promise. You're safe now. I'm not going to hurt you."

She backed away. "You're not going to get a fucking chance," she snarled. "Martin!" she screamed. "I'm in the gully."

"No!" Sam shouted.

With another scream, Jo ran. The ground was uneven and after four or five strides she put her foot on a stone that shifted sideways. There was a sudden flare of pain in her ankle but then she heard Sam behind her and kept running.

"It wasn't me," he said but didn't shout it.

She ran but he caught her arm and pulled her to one side. She let him guide her, then, as they slowed, turned and scratched at his face. He put his hands up to defend himself and she caught her thumb against the tripod of the camera. The pain lanced through her wrist and he pushed her back against the rocks.

"Stop," he said with quiet aggression. She kicked for his balls but he stepped back. "Jo, I'm not going to hurt you."

"You fucking liar." She took a deep breath and he clamped a hand over her mouth.

"Trust me," he said. "I don't want to do this but I have to because you need to believe it wasn't me."

His hand wasn't pressed tightly and she moved her head slightly to create a gap. She bit down on the edge of his palm. He shrieked and let go of her. She shoved him away but he kicked out at her foot and she fell. He knelt and pulled her onto her back and leaned in so his face was close to hers.

"It wasn't me," he insisted.

"So why are you down here?" she asked, gasping for breath.

"Because I'm trying to help you; to help both of us. Tony attacked you. Didn't you see him?"

Why was he lying now she was at his mercy? "I didn't see him because he wasn't there."

Sam shook his head. "We've got to get out of here, especially with all that screaming you did."

"Once Martin hears me, he'll come and help."

"I'm sorry, Jo," he said sadly, shaking his head.

"What?" She felt a jolt of fear. "Is Martin okay?"

Chapter 36

Martin, One Week Ago

Martin spent the rest of the day after Sandy threatened him thinking about Olivia, and his nose burned with the unshed tears he was constantly on the verge of. He saw the beauty of her smile, the sparkle in her eyes and her tinkling laugh. He thought of her utmost trust in him and the way she said 'I love you, Dad.'

He also imagined Sandy breaking her leg in enough places that she wouldn't walk properly for the rest of her life and that made him throw up.

* * *

He was driving home and trying to decide whether to throw himself on the mercy of Tommy McLain or drive into a bridge support when his phone rang.

"Hey, boss."

Martin felt a rush of hate like pure poison. "Fuck you, Gordy."

"What's that for?"

"I had a visit today from Sandy and he told me what would happen if I defaulted on my loan repayment."

"Shit. I'm sorry, boss. I didn't know."

"You never seem to know, that's always your fucking problem, Gordy. All of this is your fault."

"Did he threaten you?"

"No, it was worse than that. He's going to hurt Olivia." Martin took a deep breath and exhaled slowly. "I promise you, Gordy, that if anything happens to her then I'm going to do exactly the same to you."

"Well, you can try," Gordy said. "But I was ringing to say I might have more bad news for you."

Martin laughed, without humour. "How could that even be possible?"

"Hear me out, okay? Where are you?"

"Coming into town."

"Okay, meet me in The Rising Sun in ten minutes."

* * *

Gordy was in the same booth and waved as if he didn't have a care in the world. Martin dug his nails into his palms to stop the urge to smash Gordy's head into the wall.

There were two pints on the table and he pushed one across as Martin sat down.

"Thanks for coming, boss."

"You told me you had more bad news."

"Before I tell you, though, what did Sandy say?"

Martin told him, as concisely as possible, about the confrontation. He particularly liked Gordy's sour look when Sandy pointed out the man had no close family to threaten. "Now what's the news? Has McLain put up our interest payments?"

"Nothing like that. I just want to show you something." Gordy took out his phone then tapped the screen before sliding the handset across the table. "Have a look."

Martin pulled the phone towards him and looked at a photograph of Jo in a street with wet hair. Just behind her was a tall bald man with a beard. "Why were you stalking Jo?"

"I wasn't. I was coming down the road behind the Newborough Centre as she went into Ratty's coffee shop with that bloke. I was curious so I hung around. I take it by the fact that you haven't said something like 'oh that's her friend or brother or colleague' that you don't know him."

"I don't, but she's got wet hair. Maybe he's someone she knows from her swimming group."

"Keep looking."

The next picture showed Jo and the mystery man inside the coffee shop. They were sitting very closely at a table, laughing. Martin could feel his blood racing. There might be a perfectly innocent explanation for this but he couldn't, for the moment, think what it was. She'd never mentioned anyone other than Carole from swimming and he'd met most of her work colleagues at various functions and this bloke didn't look at all familiar.

The man was talking in the next picture and Jo was paying rapt attention to him. If he'd seen anyone else looking that way, he would have assumed they were in love. His stomach turned over at the thought that after all this he now had to deal with Jo being unfaithful. After she'd had the gall to ask him whether he had been?

"One last one," said Gordy and flicked the photo over himself.

In the last image, Jo's face was mostly obscured by the back of the mystery man's head though from the angles it was obvious what they were doing. She was kissing him. Somehow Gordy had been in the right place at the right time to catch his wife cheating.

"I feel bad for you, Martin, I really do. I couldn't believe what I saw."

"Did she see you?"

"She might have done but she's never seen me before, has she? I only know what she looks like because you had that photo of her on your desk in the office."

Martin felt weak and powerless and ill and angry, all at once. Jo's betrayal felt like a dagger being pushed between his ribs.

"I didn't know whether to say anything to you," said Gordy softly. "But I thought you deserved to know."

"Thanks," Martin muttered. It felt like his world was slipping away a little more each day.

Chapter 37

"We have to get moving," Sam said. He held out a hand for her.

"I'm not going anywhere until you tell me about Martin."

"I'll have to show you because you won't believe me if I tell you. Now get up."

He pulled her to her feet and, without letting go of her hand, ran as quickly as he could along the uneven surface.

The gully took a couple of slow twists and turns until they came to a pile of what looked like old rails and sleepers that had long since been claimed by nature.

"Here will do," Sam said and ducked down behind the vine and leaf-encrusted metalwork. He pulled Jo into a squat beside him then pressed some buttons on the back of the GoPro. "I daren't turn the volume up so you'll have to listen carefully."

"You filmed Tony attacking me?"

"Not quite," he said grimly and pressed play.

Jo squinted at the back of the GoPro screen and was thankful the image was crisp enough she could see what she was watching.

Uneven brickwork filled the screen and then she heard Martin's voice.

"You have to go back," he said.

The camera moved past a rotted window frame and lost focus for a moment then it was looking into the hut. Martin stood by the door with his hand on the frame as he looked out towards the gullies. Tony stood beside him and Jo realised with horror that Tony was leaning on the big branch he'd lashed out at her with.

"Oh no." Jo put her hands to her face as Tony hefted the branch. Surely Sam wasn't going to show her husband being killed?

Chapter 38

Martin, One Week Ago

"How do you feel, boss?"

"Like shit," Martin said. He stared at the tabletop. "How would you feel in the same situation?"

"Angry, sad, let-down, take your pick. But what if I had a plan?"

"A plan? Jo aside, all the trouble I'm in now is down to you. I ought to fucking kill you rather than listen to any suggestions."

Gordy held his hands up in surrender. "I'll cop to the fact I shouldn't have called you when Norris found us gambling, but you decided to hit him, I didn't. Just like you decided to borrow money from Mr McLain and bet on the boxing match."

"Oh, piss off," Martin said, even though he knew Gordy was right. He might have opened the doors, but Martin chose to step through them.

"But now you know about Jo, and Olivia's life has been threatened."

"Does your plan keep her safe?

"Yes."

"I trusted you before and you let me down." Martin took a long drink. "What's so different this time?"

Gordy shrugged. "If this doesn't keep Olivia safe then I won't put up a fight if you want to kill me."

"Fine," said Martin. "Now tell me."

"You said the other day that you got a letter reminding you about your life assurance."

"Uh-huh." Martin shook his head. "But you said that even if I die McLain will come after his money."

"True enough. But what if the money was paid out to you?"

"Paid out to…?" His disbelief was quickly replaced by anger and Martin was on his feet. Gordy held his hands up but Martin slapped them away and punched him. Gordy recoiled. "You wanker. I wish I'd never stood up for you."

Gordy slipped out of the booth and Martin reached for him. Gordy grabbed his elbow and pinched it hard, pushing Martin back down into his seat. Gordy leaned in close, his lips tight against his teeth. "Sit down and shut up, okay? If you touch me again, I will fucking kill you because you're out of your depth and I'm trying to help. You're not in charge, Tommy McLain is."

"I'm not going to hurt my wife, Gordy. That's insane."

"Well, I reckon you have a fairly clear choice. You either save your daughter, who hasn't done a thing wrong, or you save the woman who does this behind your back."

"Not much choice," Martin said.

"That's what I thought."

"So where do I go from here? I can't kill her and even if I could and the police figure it out, I won't get the pay-out and Olivia will still be in danger."

"What if Jo was killed and you weren't involved?"

"You mean hire someone?"

"No need. I have to pay off my own debt, Martin. If you give me half the insurance payout, I'll do it."

"You?"

"Why not? I've thought about it a lot since I took those pictures. There are plenty of dangerous places where an accident is just waiting to happen. And if a friend is there to help things along, those accidents might be more likely."

"What do you mean? Would you throw her off a bridge?"

"Close," said Gordy, "but not quite. Have you ever been camping?"

"A few times, back in the early days."

Gordy pulled the phone back towards him and his fingers danced across the screen before he slid it back. "How about this? Things have been a bit difficult for you two over the past few weeks and you're feeling bad, so you offer to take her away." He gestured towards the screen. "There's a hike and then an overnight stay in a luxury spa."

"I don't even know where Irchester Flow is."

"It's in the Northumberland Country Park. It's like a sheer cliff face. You take her up there, I push her over the edge, Bob's your uncle and we're suddenly rich enough that we can pay off McLain and start again."

Martin looked at Irchester Flow and the sheer cliff face and felt ill. He loved Jo, they'd been together a long time, but he couldn't shake that image where she gazed lovingly into her mystery man's eyes. Maybe things had been going sour for a long time. Did she still love him?

"What are you thinking, boss?"

"I'm wondering if she's about to walk away from our marriage."

"Or," Gordy said softly, "maybe she was never going to tell you about this? Have you considered that this maybe isn't the first time it's happened? What if she's been cuckolding you for years? Maybe she's been treating you like a fool for a long time and playing around when you're not looking."

"No," said Martin. He didn't want to believe it even if what Gordy was saying didn't sound like lies. Had she been cheating on him for years? He remembered how she looked when she'd asked him if he was unfaithful. Was she mocking him then? "This is ridiculous. That's not Jo at all."

"Why not? She thought you were cheating on her. Just because you were faithful doesn't mean she was."

He sounded so reasonable and if he hadn't seen the photographs Martin would have dismissed Gordy out of hand. But he had seen the photographs and he couldn't deny them. "I just can't believe it."

Gordy shrugged. "If you ask me, boss, I don't see you have much choice. It's your daughter or your wife who, whatever you might think, was getting very close to a mystery man in a coffee shop. If you organise a trip for next week, we can speak to Mr McLain and promise him full payment, plus interest and a bonus. He might even make Sandy forget about Olivia."

It was a terrible choice, but it made up Martin's mind. "How will you do it?"

"Why don't I come on the hike with you? She doesn't know me."

"But she'll have heard me talking about you, Gordy."

"Who said you have to call me Gordy?" He smiled and drank some more of his pint. "My middle name's Anthony, so why don't you call me Tony?"

Chapter 39

The video continued and Jo felt a chill sweep across her shoulders.

"We need to make sure," said Martin. "No more fuck-ups."

Jo's eyes widened. Had she heard correctly?

"She went over headfirst," said Tony.

"Did you check?" Martin's voice sounded thick and choked as if he was fighting back tears.

"How would I check? If I leaned over, I might have fallen in myself."

Martin cleared his throat. "We have to check because we won't have any more opportunities."

Realisation crept over her with a malignant touch that made her shudder.

"I think I deserve more out of this deal," said Tony.

Martin faced him and Jo could see he was angry. "Are you fucking joking? If you'd done it right on the Devil's Step and then at Irchester Flow we wouldn't be here now and we'd have witnesses."

"I didn't realise that bimbo was going to keep getting in the way. I mean how the fuck was I supposed to know, in the dark, it was her wearing Jo's jacket?"

"Because you're not paying attention. We're right at the end and you're still not checking things."

Jo felt cold in her bones at Martin's callousness. What had she ever done to deserve this?

"Anyway," Tony said. "You don't have any choice. You owe me more because I have voice notes and stuff written down that says you do."

"You're trying to blackmail me?"

"Not trying, mate. I'm a realist. You've never done this before, but I have and you need to protect yourself. Now let's go and make sure about Jo, then find Sam and fit him up for it."

The camera pulled away then and the remainder of the video was a blur of trees, undergrowth and Sam's feet as he ran along the path. Jo watched in horrified silence.

"I'm sorry you had to see that," he said.

None of it seemed possible even though she'd watched it. "Did you manage to upload this to the cloud?"

"No, still no bars."

"Maybe you'll find one if you get out to the quarry."

"That's what I thought."

"So we need to get going," she said. She felt shell-shocked and sick and her throat was dry. Why was Martin doing this?

"Where's the quarry?"

"That way," she said and pointed over his shoulder. "I saw a sign back there near the clearing." She paused and listened. The faint sound of running footsteps came to her. "How did you get down into the gully?"

"A little further back," Sam said and jerked a thumb over his shoulder. "I'll show you."

They made their way quickly along the gully and now she could hear Martin and Tony talking. After what felt like ages the ground seemed to rise slightly.

"Up here," said Sam and pointed to a thick tree whose roots were tangled around several of the rocks on the gully wall. He used them as footholds and handholds and she followed him up to the path.

Martin and Tony's voices sounded much louder now they weren't being muffled by the acoustics of the gully walls.

They hadn't run far when Martin called "Jo!"

The rage in his voice scared her. He was a hundred yards or so behind them. "What're you doing with that lanky piece of shit? He tried to kill Tony."

"Why are you doing this, Martin?" she shouted over her shoulder.

"I'm trying to protect you," he called. "We've been searching for you."

"You're a liar, Martin Harper."

"And now he's got nothing to lose," said Sam.

Chapter 40

Jo ran as fast as she could along the path but it still sounded like Martin and Tony were getting closer all the time. Sam kept pace with her, but his breathing was laboured.

The path took a meandering turn and, almost hidden in the trees, she spotted another sign warning about the steep drop to the quarry.

"Jo!" shouted Martin. "Stop! It doesn't have to be like this."

A felled tree lay across the path and she nimbly jumped it after shouting a quick warning to Sam. She hoped Martin fell over it.

Jo pushed herself harder and ran past a sign on the edge of the path that showed a stick man falling off a cliff with the words 'STEEP DROP'. She slowed as the path took a sharp turn and then she was out of the trees and on a narrow path a few feet wide. Beyond it was nothing. She pulled up sharply, but her momentum was too great. Just as the horrific realisation hit that she was going to run straight into the quarry, Sam grabbed her elbow and pulled her down to the left. She landed hard and pushed her hands into the dirt and pebbles to act like brakes. She slid into a tuft of grass that stopped her dead. The drop was inches ahead.

The quarry spread as far as she could see to the left. The path they were on appeared to run from one end to the other and there was a high ridge off to the right that seemed to bridge the two sides. She leaned over the edge and looked down past a rock face to a steep grassy incline that led into the quarry base. There were a lot of bushes and small trees dotted around. On the other side were more trees and two large areas of scree that reached at least halfway up the incline.

"Shit," said Sam as he got to his feet and helped her up.

Martin and Tony were making a lot of noise in their pursuit, and she knew they'd reach the quarry within moments. She tried to fight back the panic and calm her racing mind to think clearly.

"We have to split up," she decided.

"Are you insane?"

"No. You go to the right and up onto the high ground. If you're going to find a signal it's more likely to be there."

He leaned over to look down at the drop. "You're not going into the quarry, are you?"

"No, I'm going to the left. There's two of them and two of us so we'll split them up. Whichever one of us makes it through the quarry keeps going to Hadley Hall and calls the police."

"This isn't going to work, Jo."

"I know," she said and patted his arm. "Now fuck off."

He looked unsure so she gave him a shove then ran in the opposite direction. The path was packed earth and clear of any branches and she couldn't see too many rocks either. She glanced into the quarry occasionally but the drop past the cliff face to the incline must have been ten feet or more, so that route was definitely a last resort.

"Fuck!" Martin's cry echoed around her and she slowed to a trot then turned. She was further from the opening than she'd expected and there must have been a hundred yards between them.

"Jo!" he screamed as he looked from her to Sam. The anger rippled his voice and, for the first time in her life, she was terrified of her husband.

Sam looked to be close to the high ridge now. Martin said something to Tony and then took off towards Sam. Tony came at her.

Jo ran again and sadness tinged her fear. If Martin had come for her, despite everything she now knew, there might have been a chance to talk some sense into him. That wouldn't work with Tony. He didn't know her; he was being paid to hurt her and that was the end of it. All she could do was run.

Tony cried out and she glanced over her shoulder. His longer stride had closed the gap between them, but he'd slipped on something and was struggling to keep his balance. She didn't slow down and he was soon after her again.

She couldn't see the end of the path but had the horrible idea he would catch her before she reached it. What could she do?

Jo looked into the quarry. The drop was much the same here, but she was now almost opposite one of the scree slopes. Maybe that was the only option she had.

"I've got a signal!" Sam yelled.

Jo glanced over her shoulder again and saw Martin was almost on the ridge himself. Sam ignored him as he held his phone high.

"Sam!" she screamed.

Martin clattered into him. Both men went over in a tumble then Martin pulled Sam to his feet and grabbed for something. Sam turned his shoulder, but Martin threw a series of punches. The younger man tried to protect himself but doubled over as Martin punched him in the belly then pushed him back. Sam's arms windmilled as he struggled for balance and then he fell out of sight into the quarry.

Jo felt sick and stopped, hands on her knees as she tried to catch her breath. It was all over.

Tony slowed down and walked towards her, breathing heavily and holding his sides.

"Why are you doing all this?" she asked.

He put his hands in the small of his back and stretched. "Because I'm getting paid."

"To kill me?"

Tony grinned. "Yeah. Good, isn't it?"

"No," she said. "There was never anyone in the trees, was there?"

"Nope," he said and grinned. "Made you think there was though, didn't I?"

Jo looked down into the quarry and the drop made her feel queasy. She stepped right to the edge.

Tony's grin slid away. "What're you doing?"

"Martin will catch up with me even if I outrun you."

"I'd say so," he said.

"So, I haven't got a choice," she said and jumped.

Chapter 41

Jo cleared the rock face and the incline rushed towards her. She bent her knees as she landed but the shock of impact rippled through her knees and thighs. Her teeth clacked together and she grunted in pain.

Momentum carried her forward and she tucked her shoulder in and rolled a couple of times. A tangle of bramble snagged her ankles and stopped her progress by yanking her legs back painfully.

Dazed, she tried to unhook the thorns from her trousers. Several pierced her skin until her fingertips were sticky with blood. She kept working and looked up at the lip of the quarry. Tony leaned over and watched her with a look of open-mouthed shock.

Once she'd freed herself of the thorns, Jo got slowly to her feet. Her left leg felt fine but the moment she put too much weight on her right leg something clicked in her knee and pain shot down to her shin. She gritted her teeth and hobbled down the incline as best she could, turning side-on to try and stop herself from moving too quickly.

"No!" shouted Tony. "For fuck's sake, you bitch, why won't you just die?"

She kept moving and tried to avoid the worst of the rockfall so as not to twist her ankle. If she became incapacitated now, she really was finished.

"Martin?" Tony shouted. "She's down in the quarry."

Jo glanced at Martin. He was sitting on the edge and glaring at her; then he turned around and let his legs dangle. He was coming after her.

She tried to move faster.

Tony cried out and she turned to see him drop past the cliff face. He landed hard and she heard his breath woof out. He rolled onto his side making gulping and choking sounds.

The path ran for another thirty feet or so to the bottom of the quarry and Jo rushed down it as quickly as she dared.

She reached the bottom without somehow falling over and took a moment to catch her breath. She was on a wide, grassy track that led off in either direction. Small trees sprouted on either side but none of them looked like they would provide enough cover for her to hide behind. With her right leg injured, she wasn't going to be able to make good time and even if Tony was hurt badly there was still Martin to consider. She couldn't just stand here trying to make a decision.

Jo looked up at the other side of the quarry. The scree bed was an almost-perfect triangle that stretched halfway up the incline. A few boulders had survived the slippage and looked like stepping stones in the mass of much smaller rocks and a few dead trees were caught up in it too. Those that had survived at the edge of the slippage had branches or parts of their trunks sheared off to leave some vicious, splintered spikes.

She had two choices and neither of them seemed good. One was to follow the path of the quarry away from the ridge and hope she didn't run into a blank wall. She didn't know if quarries were formed with easy exits and now wasn't the time to try and find out. The second option was to climb thirty or more feet of scree, and that didn't seem like a good alternative at all.

Her thoughts felt like they were being whipped in a blender and it was only hearing Tony coming down the incline that made them focus. He sounded horribly near and she knew she didn't have time to think or worry. She had to decide right now. The scree route wasn't ideal but at least there he'd be as out of place as her.

She tried to remember what Peter had said back at the Devil's Steps about moving safely on scree. It wasn't impossible, he'd said, but it was treacherous underfoot and likely to break bones. She pictured him leaping to save Gayle, as agile as a mountain goat, and the way he held her. Did he say you always had to put your weight on the back foot?

Jo tested her right leg again but still got a shooting pain when she put her weight on it. Her back foot was going to have to be her left one, then.

She took a couple of deep breaths then ran and hobbled onto the scree. She fell over straight away and the rough stones dug into her knees. She bit her lip hard enough to draw blood but got unsteadily to her feet. The scree shifted slightly with a sound like the tide receding over pebbles. Turning slightly sideways she took a step and didn't slide back.

Tony ran into the base of the quarry but didn't stop and came straight at her. He jumped onto the scree and she felt it move. He scrambled and went to his knees, his hands buried in the stones. She kept moving as best she could, taking sideways steps and keeping her weight on her good foot. Her progress was far too slow.

"I'm going to catch you," he shouted. "Why make this harder on yourself?"

She reached the first boulder and gratefully climbed onto it. Her legs felt wobbly on the sure surface. She ran onto the next part of the scree, aiming for the next boulder which was perhaps six feet away.

Tony was slipping and shouting a lot but she daren't turn around to see where he was. Instead, she tried to shut him out and keep up a steady pace. Her legs ached and the pain in her right knee was getting worse.

He cried out and there was a roar of stones. She risked a glance and watched as he pulled himself onto the first boulder. His clothes were white with dust and his parka was ripped. He'd cut his head and there was blood in his hairline.

She turned her attention back to the scree. Tony shouted something but she kept looking ahead and took a few steps until the next boulder was only just out of reach. The stones shifted and she dropped back slightly. Tony's scrambling footsteps echoed around so if he'd jumped off the boulder, he must be close enough to grab her.

There was no time to waste. She threw herself towards the boulder and caught the side of it. She pulled herself up. The top of it was covered in small, jagged stones. If she turned her ankle on any of them, she was done for. Ahead was another ten feet or so of scree and then it was the edge of the grassy incline leading to the top. She was so nearly there.

Something brushed her ankle and she shrieked.

Tony laughed.

Jo got to her feet. He was so close that her only chance was to run and try to jump towards the next boulder. Running purely on fear and adrenaline, she took a step and her left foot came down heavily on a stone. She kicked back and Tony cried out. There was a heavy thud and the scree made a noise like running water.

She turned to see him sliding quickly on his back past the first boulder. There was a fresh, deep gash on his forehead and she wondered if that had been caused by the projectile she had kicked back.

He clawed at the stones to stop his descent but there was nothing he could do other than manage to sit up. He hit one of the splintered trees hard and cried out in agony. She put her hands to her mouth but couldn't look away. The branch had run itself through his side and pinned him to the spot.

'It wasn't my fault,' she told herself. 'It wasn't my fault.'

"You fucking bitch," he shouted and his face creased with pain. He tried to move but that made him cry out in agony.

He was impaled and that meant she was now clear to get away. After one last look to make sure he wasn't moving she turned to make her way up the last of the scree.

"Don't come up here," said Martin as he leaned over the edge. "If you do, I'm going to be forced to hurt you."

Chapter 42

Her emotions were as ragged as her breathing and each word cut her like a blade. "Why do you want to hurt me, Martin?"

He bit his lower lip hard. "Because the only choice I had was a terrible one."

"What are you talking about?"

"You and me." He looked one way then the other as if trying to find a way down to her. She glanced over her shoulder to make sure Tony wasn't moving. If Martin did come for her, then she was going to have to navigate the scree and take her chances.

"You and Livvy," he said.

That surprised her. "What has Olivia got to do with any of this? Are you going to hurt her, too?"

"What?" he demanded. "No, of course I'm not and I'm going to make sure she never finds out about this." He got to his feet and stood right on the edge. "This was so much easier when I thought you were fucking that guy."

"What guy?" She was struggling to keep up with his train of conversation.

"You were seen, Jo. Actions have consequences and when I was given my choice, that's what I based it on."

"I didn't give you any ultimatum to force you to make a choice."

He laughed as he moved off to her left. "You didn't have to," he said. "I saw you in that coffee shop. I saw you with *him*." He spat the word as if it was sour.

How was that possible? And whatever he'd seen of her in Ratty's with Tim, he'd clearly got the wrong end of the stick. "Whatever you think you saw it absolutely wasn't consensual." The words didn't carry the weight she wanted them to. "You didn't see me having an affair, Martin. You saw me trying to fight the bastard off because he was assaulting me."

"Well, I know that now," he shouted. "Jesus Christ, Jo. Why did you have to tell me about him? If you'd just kept your fucking mouth shut, then I would still think you'd been having an affair with him and this would be so much easier to do."

He sounded angry but he looked frightened and that scared her. Tears burned the backs of her eyes, but she was determined not to cry in front of him.

"Martin," she said, trying to think around the confusion fogging her mind. "You don't have to do anything."

"Like we could pretend all of this never happened? All this fucking death? There's no chance you could look the other way."

"Sam recorded you and Tony talking. He showed it to me and he'll show it to the police."

"That fucking kid won't be telling anybody anything."

Had Martin really killed him as well? "What did you do to him?"

"Nothing. I didn't have to because the stupid shit fell into the quarry."

"He found a signal, I heard him. He uploaded everything."

"He didn't have time. I smashed his phone and that fucking GoPro into pieces." He held out his hands. "And here we are."

If that were true, then she was properly on her own and that cleared her mind. It was all on her now and she had to figure out how to survive this insanity. "So, did you kill Gayle by mistake? What about poor old Peter? It was only you and Tony at the cliff edge with him when he went over. Did he fall or did you push him?"

"I didn't kill Gayle or push Peter," he said without meeting her gaze. He sat on the edge of the quarry and lowered himself carefully onto the grassy incline. She wasn't going to be able to talk him out of this and whatever he planned to do was going to happen soon.

She glanced behind her. Tony's teeth were gritted as he tried to pull himself off the branch, but it wasn't working. A bloodstain was blooming ominously on his parka.

"You don't have to do this, Martin. Please."

He bit his lip until blood ran down his chin. "For the love of God, Jo, shut the fuck up. Whatever you say won't make any difference because it's either you or Livvy."

"I don't even understand what that means."

"They were going to break her legs," he shouted, as if his patience had snapped. "Can you believe that?"

"Why would anyone want to break her legs?"

He laughed. It was loud and forced and sounded pained. He stopped it almost immediately. "You have no idea."

"So tell me. Give me an idea."

Martin wiped the blood away with the back of his hand but only smeared it onto his cheek. "I owe them money, okay? Are you happy now?"

"You owe money?" His stupidity was like a faceful of cold water and her anger swelled, burning through her veins. "So Gayle and Sam are dead and Peter's badly hurt and you're going to kill me because you fucking owe money?"

"You don't understand! I had a choice but I could never let anything happen to Livvy so you lost out, Jo. I'm sorry."

He made his way steadily down the incline until he was only a couple of feet from the edge of the scree.

Jo dropped into a crouch and grabbed a handful of stones. "Back away," she said. "If you come any nearer, I'll throw these and I'll be aiming for your eyes."

Martin picked up some stones himself. "I'm a better shot than you," he said. "And I'm pretty sure I can throw harder."

She heard someone stumble but they were out of sight on the path. Martin twisted around too.

"What the fuck?" he muttered, clearly not expecting company.

"Not part of your plan?" she asked.

He made his way up the incline. Jo gripped a stone tightly in her throwing hand as her gaze flicked between her husband and the top of the quarry. If the newcomer was an accomplice of his then she was done for. When Sam limped into view a few moments later, she felt a rush of relief. The side of his face was streaked with blood and the arm of his jacket was ripped off.

"Everything's uploaded to the cloud," he said and dropped to his knees. He coughed heavily and spat blood onto the ground.

Martin bellowed with fury. He tried to clamber up the quarry but lost his footing and slid back. He tried again. "You fucking lanky prick," he screamed.

She'd never heard him sound so angry. It was all over now and he had nothing left to lose. If he got to Sam he'd surely kill him and then come for her. Jo didn't have a choice. She took aim and threw as hard as she could.

The stone missed his head by inches and bounced off the incline. Martin turned to glare at her with wide eyes full of hatred.

She threw again and her aim was better, close enough this time he had to duck. She threw a third stone quickly and it hit him just above the ear. He howled in pain as he staggered back and touched behind his ear. He held his fingers out and she could see blood on them.

"You fucking bitch," he said with venom and threw a stone as he came towards her.

She heard it whistle past her ear and thump into a tree trunk someone off to her left. He raised his arm again and she knew she had to act quickly.

"Stay there, Martin!" she shouted.

"No. This is over now."

Jo looked around for larger stones and picked a couple up. As she bent down another missile from him whizzed into the ground just behind her.

She stood up straight, surprised at how close he was. She threw the first larger stone as hard as she could. It hit him in the thigh and he winced with the pain.

"Stay back," she warned but he kept coming, limping slightly now.

Jo threw the second stone and this one clipped his shoulder and bounced up to glance off his temple.

He stopped and stood for a moment, glaring at her, then sat down heavily. His eyes fluttered. Blood ran into them and he tried to blink it away.

"Stay there, Martin!" she called.

He was dazed and looked at her without seeming to see her. Holding another stone ready to throw, she ran up the scree as best she could, avoiding putting weight on her right leg as much as possible and keeping her eye on him. The stones shifted beneath her feet, but she pushed on and it seemed to take far too long but then she was on the grass. Her calves burned and her back was wet with sweat.

She caught her breath then rushed by Martin and pulled herself up over the edge of the quarry. Sam was sitting with his back to a tree and weakly raised a hand in greeting.

"Hey," he said. "Did you get him?"

"He's not going far." She hopped across the path and gingerly sat beside him, her knee flaring with pain. "Are you badly hurt?"

"Oh yeah," he muttered. "I fell into the quarry, you know."

"I jumped into it," she said.

"Jumped?" He laughed and pressed a hand to his side. "Don't make me laugh. I think I've broken all my ribs."

"We're going to have to get back."

"Can we just have five minutes before we do?"

"Uh-huh," she said. It seemed like a good idea to rest a while, and she looked across the quarry towards the trees.

Epilogue

They heard the helicopter a few minutes before the red and white craft flew overhead in a flurry of noise and wind.

Sam had managed to call them before Martin caught him so Jo got to her feet and hobbled towards the edge of the quarry to make herself more visible. She waved her hands over her head and shouted even though the noise of the rotors drowned out her voice.

The helicopter banked to the left then turned as if it was going to fly along the length of the quarry. It soon stopped and she wondered if the pilot had seen her, Martin or Tony.

"Hello!" The voice from the speaker seemed impossibly loud. She waved with both arms now as the helicopter turned to face her. "This is the Northumberland Mountain Rescue. We received a message from a Sam French. Is that you?"

Jo shook her head and waved her arms to indicate no and pointed towards Sam. He stuck up his thumb.

"The team on foot are about five minutes from your location and we are not going to be able to land here. If you need assistance we can winch you up but, if not, we will proceed to Smith Farm. Please give us a thumbs-up if you are okay for us to leave."

Sam stuck up his thumb immediately. Jo thought of Tony skewered on the tree and Martin with his wound, then stuck her own thumb up. She didn't feel cold for doing so because it was their fault while Peter hadn't asked for what happened to him.

The helicopter dipped its nose then turned and flew away across the trees.

Jo sat next to Sam again.

"I've never seen a helicopter that close up before," he said. "I suppose this is all quite exciting, really."

"Shame you're not filming it."

"Yeah. But if I did have a camera now it would just consist of me moaning about how much I hurt. I've never broken a rib before and it fucking kills to breathe."

She leaned back against the tree and closed her eyes. "At least we're safe now."

"I know." He was quiet for a moment. "So what the hell happened there? Why did your husband go mad?"

"I don't know," she said. "I suppose it'll all come out." She touched the string bracelet.

"Hey, that's one of Gayle's, isn't it?"

Jo opened her eyes. He was looking at her wrist as she stroked the bracelet. "Yes. She gave it to me yesterday when we were in the minibus. I get stressed about things."

"I would imagine you're feeling stressed now, aren't you?"

Jo looked out across the quarry and thought about everything that had happened in the past two days and everything that was likely to happen in the next few and realised she didn't feel stressed at all.

Heavy footsteps sounded along the path and then three men appeared wearing black trousers and red jackets. One of them, with a thick black beard and kind eyes, knelt in front of her.

"Are you Sam?" he asked.

"No, I'm Jo. He's Sam."

"Hello, Jo. I'm Tom and I'm part of the mountain rescue team. You're safe now."

"Thanks, Tom," she said and stroked the bracelet.

Acknowledgements

Mum, Sarah, Chris, Lucy and Milly; Nick Duncan, Sue Moorcroft, Julia Roberts, Jonathan Litchfield, Kim Talbot Hoelzli, Helen Welch and Caroline Lake; Steve Bacon and Wayne Parkin, my Balm Brothers; Peter Mark May and Richard Farren Barber; The Crusty Exterior and all who sail in her, along with my Con family; Ross Warren, Jim Mcleod and Penny Jones, who continue to lead the charge; everyone who's bought, read and reviewed one of my books; the entire team at The Book Folks.

David Roberts and Pippa, for the Friday night walks and various other adventures.

Alison and Matthew, who make everything worthwhile.

If you enjoyed this book, please let others know by leaving a quick review on Amazon. Also, if you spot anything untoward in the paperback, get in touch. We strive for the best quality and appreciate reader feedback.

editor@thebookfolks.com

www.thebookfolks.com

Also by Mark West

DON'T GO BACK

Beth's partner Nick can't quite understand why she acts so strangely when they return to her hometown for the funeral of a once-close friend. But she hasn't told him everything about her past. Memories of one terrible summer will come flooding back to her. And with them, violence and revenge.

ONLY WATCHING YOU

After separating from her cheating husband, Claire begins to feel watched. She nearly gets run over and someone daubs a hangman symbol on a wall near her house. As letters begin to get added to the game, she'll need to find the identity of her stalker before they raise the stakes.

THE HUNTER'S QUARRY

Young single mother Rachel has no idea why an assassin is trying to kill her. Have they confused her with someone else? Did she do something wrong? Whatever the answer, it looks like they'll carry on trying unless she can get to safety or turn the tables on them. But first she'll have to find out what they want from her.

STILL WATERS RUN

A short holiday at the end of summer should be a chance for sixteen-year-old Dan and his recently divorced mother to unwind. Yet despite quickly striking up new friendships, their break takes a nasty turn when a holiday worker is murdered. Dan becomes embroiled in events. Can he get out or is he in too deep?

All FREE with Kindle Unlimited and available in paperback!

Other titles of interest

FOR MY OWN GOOD by Vanessa Garbin

Mary is on meds which make her forgetful. It's been like this ever since an incident when her baby was injured. Now her husband is being way over-protective. He insists Mary stays indoors, for her own good. He's hired a nanny. But Mary can't remember her child getting hurt. And if she can't recall what happened, how can she make things right?

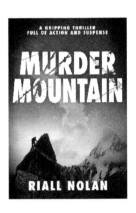

MURDER MOUNTAIN by Riall Nolan

Wanted by the FBI and hiding out on a remote island in
the Pacific, Peter Blake has an unwelcome visit. He's been
rumbled by a man who "trades in information" and the
price for not being handed over to the authorities is to use
his mountaineering experience to lead a team on a
dangerous mission to recover a fallen satellite. If he fails, it
will cost him his life.

All FREE with Kindle Unlimited and available in paperback!

www.thebookfolks.com